happenstance

Happenstance
Jamie McGuire

Copyright © 2014 Jamie McGuire

ISBN: 1505357608

ISBN 13: 9781505357608

happenstance

*a novella series
part one*

JAMIE MCGUIRE

For Lori Bretch.

table of contents

1.

"GO HOME. TURN OFF THE lights. And kill yourself."

Erin Alderman glowered at me, pure hatred in her beautiful honey brown eyes. She was spearheading a group of nine cheerleaders on the other side of a small, rectangular window. But the glass wasn't the only thing that separated us.

Nine pairs of eyes danced between each other and me in my black apron splattered with chocolate milkshake and fudge sauce. They were enjoying the show, but not one of them looked directly at me.

Erin Masterson, Erin Alderman's best friend and co-captain of the cheer squad, was holding the banana split Blizzard I'd just made for her, with vengeance in her eyes. She was as beautifully put together as her best friend, but instead of long, flowing golden hair like her friend, she had long, flowing chestnut hair. "I said with walnuts on top. You have a simple function: put ice cream in a bowl, cup, or cone, and mix ingredients. If you can't perform a minimum wage job at a Dairy Queen at seventeen years old, how do you expect to operate in your daily adult life? You should give up now, Erin. Die with dignity."

Erin Masterson wasn't speaking to her best friend. She was speaking to me, Erin Easter, the third Erin in our senior class. They weren't always my enemies. In kindergarten and first grade, we tried to spend every waking moment together; our teachers and parents came up with nicknames to eliminate confusion. Erin Alderman was known as Alder. Erin Masterson was Sonny. My name was simple: Easter. The three of us didn't share only names, we also shared a birthday: September first. They went home with their parents, who were country club members and would eventually be heads of the Free Masons and the PTA, and I went home with my mother, who was barely twenty and had no one to help, not even my father.

Our friendship changed dramatically in fifth grade when, for reasons I'm still not sure of, I became the Erin's favorite target. Now in our senior year of high school, I mostly tried to avoid them, but they loved to visit me at the Dairy Queen where I worked on weekends and almost every day after school.

I pulled up the sliding window and poked my hand through. "I'm sorry. Hand it to me and I'll remake it."

Frankie bumped me to the side with her hip, yanked the cup out of Sonny's hand, scooped out the large chunk of brown ice cream with peanut chunks, and tossed it in the trash. She spooned in a half dozen walnuts, and handed it back. "I'm not wasting an entire cup of ice cream because your mama didn't teach you how to deal with disappointment. Get the hell on," she said, jerking her head to the side.

"I'll let my *mama* know how you feel about her parenting, *Frances*." Sonny spat out the words, making sure to call Frankie by her given name, the name she loathed. "I'm sure your litter makes you an expert."

Frankie grinned politely. "That term is for dogs, Masterson. No one but your mother calls their kids that."

The Erins glared at Frankie, and then all ten girls walked away as one unit.

"Sorry," I said, watching the cheerleaders happily jog across the street, energized from their confrontation.

Frankie frowned and perched her hand on the curve of her hip. "Why are you apologizing? I've told you a hundred times, but I'll tell you again. Stop taking crap from those harpies. It only makes them worse. Ignoring does not work with bullies like that. Believe me, I know."

"Only three months left, though," I said, washing the sticky milk and sugar from my hands.

Frankie sighed and looked at the ceiling with a sigh. "I remember graduation. One of the best nights of my life. All of that freedom, just waiting to be experienced. It was all ahead of me—summer, college, turning twenty-one." The dreamy look in her eyes faded, and she cleaned the counter. "One night with Shane was all it took to make it disappear. Seven years later, I'm at the same job I had in high school." She shook her head and laughed once, scrubbing a stubborn piece of dried chocolate off the counter. "I wouldn't trade my babies for the world, though."

One corner of my mouth turned up as I watched Frankie mull over the decisions that kept her at the Dairy Queen. She counted herself lucky to have a job. The oil company had moved, and all the decent paying jobs left with it, so a paycheck from the Dairy Queen was as good as anything in our struggling town.

The phone rang, and Frankie answered it. "No, Keaton, you can't eat the peanut butter out of the jar. Because I said. If you're starving, then eat a banana. Then you're not starving! I said no, and that's that. Put Nana on the phone. Hi, Mama. Okay. Same as always. How about you? Good. No, Kendra has dance at six. Kyle has T-ball at seven." She smiled. "All right. Love you, too. Bye."

She hung up and turned to me, mirroring the strange look on my face.

"Did you lose one?" I asked.

Frankie chuckled. "No. The baby's asleep, thank the lord."

She wiped the counters again, and I cleaned up the mess from making Sonny's banana split Blizzard. Our Dairy Queen was housed in one of the smallest and oldest buildings in Blackwell, a tiny speck on the Oklahoma map. The owners, Cecil and Patty, were more than happy to let out-of-towners stop to take pictures of their unique fifties-style building. Patrons could order from one of the two sliding windows in the front, or the drive-thru on the south side. There was barely room for Frankie and me to move around, and we often bumped into each other when we had a rush of customers after baseball games or during fair week. A lone shaded bench was placed on the side of the building for customers who wanted to stick around to eat their dip cones or hot dogs, but it was usually empty.

"Oh, goody. Practice is over," Frankie said, watching the various cars and trucks belonging to the baseball team back out of their spots in the gravel lot across the street. Several of them drove into the DQ and parked, a dozen sweaty boys hopped out and walked across the asphalt to my window. Frankie opened hers, and two lines formed.

Weston Gates had to lean down to look at me, his eyes meeting mine through shaggy, brown strands of hair, still wet with perspiration. His dark gray T-shirt read BLACKWELL MAROONS. The maroon lettering crackled from numerous washes during his now fourth year of high school football, basketball, and baseball. His father was a jock at Blackwell high school, too, and his mother and older sister Whitney were both head cheerleaders. Whitney was now in her second year of college at Duke University, going for her law degree, and she rarely came home. I didn't know her well, but she had beautiful, kind eyes, just like Weston.

"Just whatever, Erin. It's all good," he said with a shy smile.

"Did you just say she was good, Wes?" Brady Beck chided. "How would you know? I didn't know you've been slumming it."

The other guys chuckled and made stupid noises.

Weston's cheeks were already flushed from practice, making them look like someone had brushed a light red paint brush across them and slapped him…twice. They turned two shades darker. The rosiness of his cheeks against his emerald eyes made them appear even brighter. I'd been trying not to stare at those eyes since grade school, and once Alder had set her sights on him in eighth grade, I tried even harder.

"Ignore them, Erin. They're assholes." He choked a bit when he spoke, then he turned to cough into the crook of his elbow.

I made him a simple strawberry dip cone—extra tall, because I knew that was his favorite—took his money, and watched him drop his change in my plastic tip jar.

"Thank you," he said, taking a big bite off the top as he walked back to his truck.

The other guys weren't as polite, and most of them didn't even look me in the eye. I was used to that, though. Growing up with a mom who had seen the inside of a jail cell more than once, the other parents weren't shy about keeping their children from being corrupted by Gina Easter's daughter. My mother wasn't always so messed up though. She was Blackwell's homecoming queen in 1995. I knew that only because I'd come across the photos. She was beautiful, with her blonde bangs teased to one side and her full, healthy cheeks pushing up her big brown eyes into slits.

Like Frankie, Gina got pregnant young. Unlike Frankie, she let the resentment of trading her dreams for an unplanned baby become so unbearable, she turned to alcohol. And weed. And as the years added disappointments to the growing pile, any drug was good enough if it helped her forget what she could have been. I wouldn't have minded so much if it did numb her anger, but most nights adding a case of Keystone Light to her rage just made it worse.

Every night when Frankie shut off the lights and said her favorite phrase, I cringed, knowing it was time to go home to Gina.

"Adios bitchachos!"

"Don't forget I have a senior class meeting tomorrow after school, so I'll be a little late."

"I remember," she said, grabbing her purse and keys. She held open the door for me. "Ride?"

I shook my head. Every night she asked me, and every night I said no, which is why she barely made a question of it. I lived only five blocks behind the DQ anyway, and the first day of spring was right around the corner.

The soles of my shoes crunched the loose gravel next to the curb as I walked along the dark street. Only random areas around town had sidewalks, and the shortest path to my house wasn't one of them. A few cars drove by, but it was an otherwise quiet Thursday night. No church traffic, no game traffic. Thursdays were my favorite nights to walk home.

I climbed the concrete steps to the porch, and the screen door whined when it opened. I could hear Gina's music from the other side of the door, and hesitated just long enough to psych myself up for whatever awaited me on the other side. When the door swung open, and I saw that the living room was empty, I hurried to my room and shut the door.

The music was coming from her bedroom, down the hall from mine. I could smell the weed as soon as I walked in, so she was probably smoking and relaxing in her bed, which was always preferable to a drunken rage.

The loose strings of my apron untied easily, and I peeled off the rest of my clothes, throwing them into a full hamper. Most nights I was too tired to do laundry, so it piled up until I hauled it to the Laundromat a few blocks south of the Dairy Queen. Being alone at the Suds & Duds was creepy at night, so I preferred to wait until early Saturday afternoon. Gina was awake then, and it was a good excuse to get out of the house before work.

I slipped on an oversized, faded black T-shirt that read OAKLAND RAIDERS. I'd assumed it was my dad's, but I wasn't sure. It could have been one of the random items Gina picked up from the secondhand store. But for some reason, I liked to think it was his—whoever he was—and wearing it made the roach-infested termite palace we lived in feel a little more like home.

I sat on the green carpet in my bedroom. It was once something similar to shag, but it had become matted over the years and looked more like the pelt of a very ugly animal. I had a page of Algebra II to finish; then I crept down the hall to the bathroom, washing my face and brushing my teeth to the muffled lyrics of Soul Asylum. Gina was definitely high. "Runaway Train" was her go-to song when she scored a dime bag of weed.

Back in my room, I sat on the edge of my bed and watched my reflection in the mirror atop my dresser. They were from the second hand store, like everything else in our house. The mirror wobbled when anyone walked across my floor, and most of the dresser drawers didn't open right, but they completed their function, and that's all I needed. I brushed my dark brown hair away from my face until the brush could pass every strand without catching then smoothed it back into a ponytail.

The aging springs of my bed complained when I crawled under the covers. The ceiling fan bobbed as it turned slowly, lulling me to sleep as whatever song Gina was listening to hummed through the walls. I took a deep breath. The next day would be long. The senior class meeting was mandatory, and I dreaded going. I generally avoided school functions, just to save myself the humiliation suffered at the hands of the other Erins. Middle school taught me that any attempt to socialize was not worth the inevitable teasing and sometimes bullying that ensued. At times, teachers intervened, but mostly they didn't. The Erins, along with Brady Beck and a few of their friends, relished only one thing more than taunting me—making me cry. That always seemed to be the goal, and the more I resisted, the harder they tried. So for the last four years, I kept to school and work, and myself. I had won a scholarship, and between that and grants, I was getting the hell out of Blackwell, away from the Erins, Brady, and Gina.

I reached over and pulled the lamp string. As much as Sonny genuinely wanted me to, I wouldn't turn out the light and kill myself. I was going to rest, save my strength for another grueling day. Tomorrow would bring me one day closer to the freedom that Frankie dreamed about.

2.

THIRTY MINUTES BEFORE THE first bell rang, I adjusted my backpack and set out on my morning trek. Blackwell High School was just a few miles away, so unless something wet was falling out of the sky, the walk really wasn't that bad. It was these quiet moments between Gina and school that I savored the most—but I wouldn't miss them. I wouldn't miss anything about Blackwell, except for Frankie, her snot-nosed kids, and maybe Weston's green eyes.

Oklahoma State University's campus was just under an hour away by car, in Stillwater. The campus was small enough that I wouldn't need a car and the transit system would take me anywhere else I needed to go nearby. But I had to figure out a way to OSU. The acceptance letter came in the mail a couple of weeks before, and I celebrated alone, jumping up and down in the kitchen. Gina didn't know. I hadn't even told Frankie. I didn't want to jinx it.

Half a block before I reached the school, the sky opened, and a cold spring rain poured down. My pace broke out into a sprint. I didn't want my shoes to slosh and draw attention more than my sopping hair already would.

Once inside, I walked straight to the east wing bathroom. It was next to the office, so teachers were more likely to be in there. Sure enough, Mrs. Pyles was drying her hands under the automatic dryer.

She greeted me with a smile, but once she recognized how drenched I was, her expression changed. "Oh, Erin!" She yanked paper towels from the holder and handed them to me. "Didn't you know it was going to rain today?"

I shook my head. "I had a feeling. Hoped I could make it here before it started."

She helped me slide my backpack to the floor and took my jacket, holding it under the electric dryer. "I've given you my number a dozen times. Why won't you call me?"

I shrugged. "I like to walk."

She frowned. "Next time the weather man calls for precipitation before school, I'm going to be parked in front of your house."

"Please don't," I said. "You'll embarrass Gina. She won't like it."

"I don't care."

I pushed the silver button and leaned beneath the dryer. "I just have a couple more months. It's not worth it."

Mrs. Pyles shook her head, her bright blue eyes heavy with sadness. "I haven't done enough for you, have I?"

"You've done plenty. See you in class." I left her alone in the bathroom.

Mrs. Pyles cared about her students, and she'd asked me so many times if everything was okay at home. It had to be so frustrating to be in her position. Gina had a bad temper, and she was a mean drunk, but DHS had been called a few times before and they could never find a good enough reason to save me. Mrs. Pyles always seemed to be in a mood the day after DHS made a surprise visit to my home. It had occurred to me that she might be the one reporting Gina, but I'd never asked. It didn't matter, and no one should have to answer for trying to protect someone.

First period was Mrs. Merit's Advanced Biology class, and I shared it with Brady Beck. Four students sat at assigned seats around five round tables with black counter tops, carved with initials and pluses or hearts, the abbreviation "Sr." followed by every year since 1973, and inappropriate pictures.

I sat in my seat at the middle table and watched other students filter in. Brady and his friend Brendan ran in just before the bell rang, sliding into their seats with shit-eating grins on their faces. They were both at the corner table. Brady had traded spots with Andrew at the beginning of the year so he could face me and mouth things like *whore* or *skank*. Sometimes he said it out loud, but Mrs. Merit wasn't one of the teachers that minded if I was bullied.

Once the shrill beeping of the bell ended, Mrs. Merit offered them an annoyed smile, and began setting up for the lesson.

Sara Glen sat across from me at our table. She was only chatty with me when she wanted to tell me what rumor was spreading about me that day, like when Brian Grand began a discussion in health class about how disgusting it was that I wore the same dirty jeans every day.

I had two pair that I'd found at the Second Hand, and they looked nearly identical. Once I'd spilled something on them two days in a row, and because of work, I didn't have time to take them to the Laundromat. That was when Brian noticed, and I couldn't argue, because it was true.

"Erin," Sara whispered. She put her elbows on the table and leaned in. "I heard you got fired from the Dairy Queen for spitting in Sonny's ice cream. People are saying you have AIDS and were trying to give it to her out of spite."

"AIDS. That's a new one," I said, doodling in my notebook.

"So it's not true?"

"No."

"Which part?"

"All of it."

Sara seemed satisfied, so she returned her gaze to the teacher.

"Spring break is the week after next, people," Mrs. Merit said. "We have a mid-term test. I'll hand out the study guide a week from today. Look it over."

Mrs. Merit's study guides were the questions and answers, albeit worded slightly different, of the test, in order. Even though it was supposed to be an advanced class, studying consisted of memorization, so it didn't surprise me that Sara didn't know AIDS couldn't be transmitted through a little bit of spit. A percentage of the girls in our class hadn't even gotten to graduation before getting pregnant, so basic biological knowledge didn't seem to be a priority among these students. Or maybe there just wasn't enough to do besides stand around and drink at bonfire parties at the Diversion Dam or have sex.

Lunch came and went, then I had fifth period Health class—my least favorite—with the Erins. I had third period Calculus with Alder, but she didn't speak to me without her cohorts around. Brady was in fifth period, too, but he typically left me alone to pick on Annie Black, a sweet and incredibly smart junior with cerebral palsy. He did an Annie impression every time she passed him in the halls. Only a few people called him out on how disgusting he was. He was born into one of the most affluent families in Blackwell, and his parents were pillars of the community. His father had donated hundreds of thousands of dollars to the school, and his mother was a rather rabid bitch and shrieked to her good friend the superintendent whenever someone dared instruct her son on rules or common courtesy, so even the teachers tried to ignore his antics. Brady Beck had been caught vandalizing the school, drinking on school grounds, skipping class, and bullying dozens, but he never once sat through Detention. He was everything that was wrong with our little town.

I sat at my desk and waited. It was Friday, so Coach Morris didn't make us do much. He usually had us do a word find or let us read to ourselves. When we didn't have much work to do though, the Erins made themselves busy with me. It would be easy to ignore them if Weston didn't sit right behind me. But for whatever reason, when he was around, their jabs felt more humiliating.

"All right, hoodlums. Pull out a book and read. TGIF."

Ten minutes hadn't yet passed when I heard someone whisper my name—possibly my name. A few seconds later, it was louder, and I recognized the voice as Sonny's. She was trying to get my attention. I didn't dare turn around. Any hope of comprehending the words on the page in front of me was lost. I just stared at one word and hoped Sonny wouldn't catch the coach's attention.

Coach Morris perked up and nodded to the back of the class. "Yes?"

Sonny lowered her hand and sat tall in her seat with a smug expression. "I was just wondering what the school policy is on the AIDS virus."

"What do you mean?" Coach asked.

"If one of the students has tested positive for AIDS, what does the school do to protect the rest of the students?"

"Why do you ask?" The curious light in the coach's eyes had extinguished, and it was obvious that he knew Erin was up to something.

"I just heard today that one of our students has it, and everyone is nervous."

"Why?"

"Because it's contagious, and no one wants to die just because some skank wants to punish everyone else for her loose ways."

"Loose ways," Coach Morris deadpanned. "I can explain the school policy with you in detail after seventh period if you'd like."

"I have cheer," Erin said, annoyed that her plan didn't work. "I'm sure the entire class would feel better hearing what you have to say."

Coach sighed. "I think it's more likely that you're helping to spread a cruel rumor."

A collective tittering made its way through the classroom.

"That's offensive," Sonny said. "What are you again? A karmologist?"

Coach chuckled. "Kinesiologist."

"That's what I said. You'd think a graduate of health science would typically consider my concern valid."

Coach didn't hesitate. "Common sense disagrees. Read your book. No more talking."

His perceptive remark saved me from further ridicule for now, but the senior meeting after school was going to be considerably less fun.

"What are you reading?" A deep voice asked.

I barely acknowledged Weston's question, holding up the cover of my book high enough for him to see.

He nodded, waiting for me to speak. When I didn't, he offered a small smile, and sat back.

"What are you reading?" I asked.

Weston immediately leaned toward me, holding up his cover the way I had.

"Piers Anthony?"

Weston cleared his throat to stifle a cough then smiled. "I like his stuff."

I nodded. "I approve."

"Good," Weston whispered. "I was worried." After a short pause, he leaned into my ear again. "Why don't you ever talk to me in Art class?"

We had seventh period Art together, the class I looked forward to all day. Weston was in it, but more important, people like the Erins and Brady weren't. We were serious about our work, and it was the one place during the school day that I could be myself.

"I guess I was just busy."

"Are you going to be busy today?"

"Probably."

"Well, maybe I'll get lucky and you'll take a break."

I turned around to hide my grin, but not before glancing back and seeing the familiar look of hatred in Alder's eyes.

Whore, she mouthed, glaring at me.

* * *

After seventh period, I put my books in my locker and walked slowly to the east hall, the fifty-minute-long high I'd been on with Weston during Art quickly faded with each step. I dreaded seeing everyone's reaction when I walked through the door.

Brady and Brendan were sitting on top of desks, some students were looking at their phones, texting or checking social media, and the Erins were sitting at desks that were turned around to face everyone else. Mrs. Hunter, English IV teacher and senior class adviser, wasn't there yet. *Shit.*

"What are you doing here?" Alder said. I didn't answer, but that never deterred the Erins. "No one wants your opinion."

I took a seat in the back near the door and hoped Mrs. Hunter wouldn't be much longer.

Sonny feigned sympathy. "You can leave. No one gives a shit what you have to say, anyway."

"It's mandatory," I said simply. "I'm not leaving."

Sonny stood up. "You will if I make you."

"Sit down," I said.

Sonny's expression morphed from annoyance to shock to rage. "What did you say to me?"

I looked her straight in the eye. "I'm staying. Sit down."

Weston's gaze bounced from the Erins, to me, and back. Sonny took a step toward me, and Weston stood. By the look on his face, even he was surprised at his reaction.

Sonny looked at him with utter disgust. "What are you doing, Wes?"

Weston cocked his head for a moment. He took a breath and blinked a few times, clearly unhappy about being in the middle of things. "It's a mandatory meeting. No point in making her miserable over it. She probably doesn't want to be here."

"Weston!" Alder said, astonished.

Weston took a puff from his inhaler, staring his girlfriend in the eye. "Leave her alone."

Just as both Erins' mouths fell open, Mrs. Hunter breezed through the door and headed to the front of the class. "What did I miss?"

Weston sat down, and so did Sonny.

"Nothin," Sonny grumbled.

"Okay, let's get started," Mrs. Hunter said, winded. "Who wants to be in charge of the senior assembly?"

The relief that washed over me made me emotional, more than I'd been in quite a while, but I kept the tears inside, refusing to let my classmates see me cry. They would just have to be disappointed for the day.

3.

"BITCHES!" FRANKIE SAID, AS she watched soft serve feed out of the machine. "I can't believe she bowed up on you like that. What was she going to do? That's right! Nothing!"

"Are you even talking to me right now?" I asked, amused.

"I would *love* to talk to the twaterati about it. Love!"

I laughed once and shook my head, letting the mixer blades make love to the M&M Blizzard I was making. When Frankie trained me, she said it looked a lot like giving a guy a hand job. I wasn't exactly sure what that was like, but I would make someone very happy one day.

Frankie was ten customers deep when I finally arrived after the senior class meeting, and we hadn't had a break in four hours. Friday nights were always hectic, but that didn't stop

Frankie from ranting about my confrontation with Sonny.

She put her hand on her hip, and all of her weight on one leg. "I am so proud of you. For real. I think it's the first time you've ever stood up for yourself, isn't it?"

"I don't know. It wasn't really standing up for myself. I just told her that I was staying."

"And to sit her bitch ass down." She wrinkled her nose. "That part's my favorite."

Just as the sun began to set, the pace eased up a bit. The last car left the parking lot, and I began scrubbing the huge mess we'd made when we didn't have time to clean up after ourselves—or be careful—before the next rush.

A truck pulled in quickly, and I knew instantly who it was. Weston Gates was the only person in town with a lift kit and Rock Star rims on a cherry red Chevy. He hopped down and jogged over to my window. He was sweaty, still in his baseball cleats, and alone.

"Hey."

"Hey," I said, glancing over to Frankie. "What can I get for you?"

Weston watched me for a moment.

"Are you okay?" I asked.

He blinked. "Yeah. Yeah," he said, shrugging. "Are you?"

I shrugged. "I'm fine. Can I make you something?"

"Just a...whatever."

I made him a Hawaiian Blizzard and he paid, still with that expectant look in his eyes. "I'm sorry. About today."

I shook my head dismissively.

"I should have said something sooner."

"Yeah, like ten years ago," Frankie shot back.

He nodded and then walked back to his truck, but he was hesitant, as if he were leaving something unsaid.

Frankie sighed. "I shouldn't have snapped at him. He seems like a good kid."

"He is," I said, unable to stop staring as Weston climbed up into the driver's seat and shut the door.

"That was...weird."

"Yeah, I wonder what that was about?" As I watched his truck pull onto Main Street, a wide grin stretched across my face.

"I think he likes you."

The smile vanished. "What about that bizarre exchange brought you to that conclusion?"

She shrugged. "I was in high school once."

Frankie and I finished up our shift, and then closed the shop. She offered me a ride and I refused then walked home. I kept mostly to the yards of the houses along the way, to keep from being mowed down by the traffic traveling toward Main Street. That was the main drag, and on Friday nights everyone congregated at the ball fields that were straight across from the Dairy Queen.

A block from my house, a familiar engine revved from the other side of the street. I looked over to see Weston's red Chevy. His window was rolled down, and the truck was crawling along next to me. He was alone again.

"Hey," he said, his elbow poking out as he rested it on the driver's side door.

I didn't respond.

He smiled. "What are you doing?"

"What does it look like I'm doing?" I said, trying not to smile the way I had after he'd left the DQ.

"It looks like you're walking home. Do you have plans tonight?"

I narrowed my eyes at him. He knew I didn't.

"Wanna hang out?" he asked.

"Aren't your friends at the ball fields?" I already knew the answer. They were there every Friday and Saturday night if there wasn't a party. What I really wanted to know was why he was driving next to me, instead of hanging with them.

"I told them I was tired and going home."

"But you're not?"

"Well...more like bored. But then I saw you..."

I looked down. "I'm not really dressed to hang out."

"You're talking to someone who loves ice cream. You think it offends me that you're covered in it?"

I laughed.

"C'mon!" he said with a smile that had been perfected by braces. He'd only gotten them off the summer before. "I'll beg if you want me to."

"You don't have to beg," I murmured.

"What?"

I chuckled. "Fine! Just...let me change first."

"Deal!"

I pointed at him. "Park right there. I'll be out in a second." We were still half a block from my house, and I didn't want the absurdly loud glass packs of Weston's Chevy to attract Gina's attention.

Trying not to rush, I walked to my house, up the two stairs to my porch, and pulled open the door. Out of habit, I listened for Soul Asylum, but no such luck. I pushed through the door, to see Gina sitting on the stained, gold velvet couch in the living room. A ripped-open case of Keystone Light was next to her feet on the floor. She didn't even look up.

I went straight to my room, dropped my backpack to the floor, pulled off my apron, the rest of my clothes, and re-dressed. Everything I wore to work inevitably smelled like grease, so it all had to come off. I put on a black T-shirt and a pair of heather gray cotton shorts, slipped on some flip flops and grabbed my purse. My second pair of jeans was on the floor spattered with chocolate syrup. It was the day before laundry day, so even though it was a little chilly, the shorts were the only thing I had clean.

I closed my door quietly and tried to rush past Gina, but she noticed me walk by and sat up.

"Where the hell you goin'?" she asked.

"Riding around. I'll be back in a little while."

She sat back against the couch cushions. "Bring me back some cigarettes."

I nodded and hurried out the door. She would be passed out before I got back and wouldn't remember that she asked me for anything. Unfortunately I'd only learned that after wasting over a hundred dollars of my own money buying her smokes to appease her.

I stopped in the yard, half expecting Weston's truck to be gone, but there it was, in the exact spot I told him to wait. His eyes lit up, and he waved. As I made my way to his truck, he leaned over and pulled the lever, pushing the door open.

"Climb in!" he said with a sweet grin.

He wasn't kidding. I had to use the door and climb up via the running boards to reach the passenger seat. I bounced into the black leather and shut the door.

"Wow," I said.

He shrugged. "Don't be too impressed. It was my dad's."

"Better than nothing," I teased.

"Where do you wanna go?" he asked.

I smiled. "Anywhere."

Weston sucked on the straw of his enormous cherry Icee, and we bounced over the potholes and patches of Blackwell's roads, listening to the Chance Anderson Band on full blast. Within five minutes, we were outside the city limits. Weston parked at the peak of an overpass that arched over I-35, and we watched the headlights of cars and semis flow beneath us, traveling north and south.

I pushed open the passenger door and walked over to the edge. The rural overpasses didn't have rails. It was just concrete up to your belly and common sense. A chilly breeze kissed my face, so I turned around, not exactly surprised to see lightning crackling across the clouds gathering to the north.

"I love how the storms always suck the wind into them," I said.

Weston's door slammed shut, and he was standing next to me. He drank the last of his Icee, and the straw against the Styrofoam made a loud slurping sound. "I just love storms."

"So…are you going to tell me?" I asked.

Weston could barely pull his eyes away from the storm. "Tell you what?"

"Why you brought me out here?"

He shrugged. He was chewing on his straw, which I found oddly appealing. "Why not?"

"There are a hundred reasons why not. I was asking about the one reason why I'm here."

"Because I asked?"

I laughed once and looked down. "Okay. If that's the way you want to play this."

"I don't want to play this at all. I just want to sit up here and watch the storm roll in with you, without all the gossip of who's doing who, and where so-and-so is going to college. Is that okay?"

I nodded. "I can live with that."

Weston let the Chevy's tailgate down and climbed up, reaching for my hand. "Well? C'mon."

I let him help me to the bed of his truck and sat next to him, letting my legs dangle off the edge.

He nodded behind us. "I have stuff to drink in that cooler."

I shook my head. "I don't drink."

"No, like, Fanta Orange and stuff. I think I have a few Cherry Cokes and one Mountain Dew."

"How could I possibly choose? Those are all my favorites."

He smiled and reached back. "Mine, too. I'll just grab ya one." His hands fished around in the melted ice, and he pulled out a green can. "And the winner is…Mountain Dew. You must be lucky."

I popped the top. "Not so far. Thank you."

"Maybe that'll change. For both of us."

"You don't feel lucky?" I asked.

He thought about it for a moment. "You're the last person I should be talking to about my problems."

"Gee, thanks."

"I just mean that you'll think I'm being stupid. Because they're not even close to the kind of hell you go through."

I shrugged. "It's not that bad."

"If I had to endure that every day, I couldn't do it. You're pretty damn tough, Erin Easter."

He rested his arm on his knee and his chin on his fist as he stared at me. His jeans weren't pulled all the way down over his cowboy boots, and his hoodie was worn. Suddenly he didn't seem so out of reach.

Lightning from the north sky flashed in his eyes, and we both gasped.

"That was a good one," he said. "Too bad it's going to miss us."

"Good. Bad. It's all the same."

"What does that mean?" he said, smiling.

"There's an old Chinese proverb Mrs. Pyles told me once about an old Taoist farmer. I think about it a lot."

"Tell me," he said, nudging me.

"I don't remember it verbatim."

"Paraphrase then."

I took a breath. "One day, the only horse the farmer owned died. It was the only way he could plow his fields. Everyone in the village came to offer their condolences for his bad luck. The farmer said, 'We'll see.' A week later, his son came across a heard of wild horses and managed to bring home two. The village was amazed at their good fortune. The farmer said, 'We'll see.' While the son was trying to break one of the horses, he fell off and fractured both of his legs. The village doctor said he would never walk again. Villagers came to console the farmer, because this was his only son. The farmer said, 'We'll see.' Soon after, war ravaged the land. All of the able-bodied sons of the village were collected for the draft. The farmer's son was the only one left behind. None of the boys who went to war returned."

"Wow."

"Yeah. She told me that in ninth grade. It's always stuck with me."

"I like it. It's…applicable."

I arched an eyebrow.

He chuckled, and I did, too. Thunder rolled, grumbling all around us, and the wind picked up.

Weston lifted his chin. "Smells like rain." His cell phone chirped. He took one look at it and stuffed it back into the front pouch of his hoodie.

I took a sip of my Mountain Dew. "Erin?"

"Yep."

"You've never seemed like…"

"Her type?"

"No," I said, chuckling and shaking my head. "Not at all."

"I guess I'm not. My parents sure like the idea of it."

"Oh."

"Yeah. They like the idea of a lot of things." He leaned back, using his arm as a pillow as he looked up at the sky.

I did the same, noticing that the only patch of clear sky was directly above us. "Will they want you home any time soon?"

"Nope. Do you need to be?"

"Nope."

Weston took a deep breath, and we just lay there for the longest time. Neither of us felt the need to fill the silence as we watched the storm clouds slowly close in on the stars above.

4.

WALKING INTO THIRD PERIOD gave me pause. A familiar face with kind blue eyes and perfectly glossed lips looked up at me. "Hi, there. Come on in."

Julianne Alderman stood behind Mr. Barrows's desk, nervously shuffling papers. "Oh, my. I'm not very good at this."

I just watched her as the other students filled the desks. They barely noticed her and were talking and laughing loudly.

"What the...what are you doing here?" Alder said, frozen in the doorway. Her eyes were wide.

Julianne smiled. "Obviously they were very desperate for a substitute."

Alder rolled her eyes and scampered to her seat, ducking down. "This is so freaking embarrassing, Mother. Jesus."

"Erin," Julianne warned, although there wasn't even a glimmer of anger in her eyes.

Gina would have climbed over the desk at me by then.

Julianne's shiny brown hair bounced as she walked around the classroom, passing out papers. As a child, I fantasized about what it would be like to grow up with a mother like her. Alder always showed up to school on Halloween in a gorgeous, homemade princess costume, complete with a pink pointy hat and ribbon flowing from the top. Sam and Julianne were always at the games that Alder cheered at to support her, wearing buttons on their jackets featuring her cheer picture. For her sixteenth birthday, they bought her a shiny new Honda Accord, which she hated. She didn't know she was lucky to take those things for granted, that everyone didn't get the same love and attention that she did, so I didn't really hold it against her. Even though I wanted to.

Julianne sat in Mr. Barrows's chair and grinned, her blue eyes sparkling. We had similar coloring, the same heart-shaped face, similar dark hair and blue eyes, so I hoped I still looked as young and beautiful as she did when I was her age.

Alder groaned. "What is this?"

"It's your assignment," Julianne said. "Mr. Barrows said you would know what to do, so get to it, guys. You have to finish before the end of the period. No one can take this home."

Everyone but me grumbled, and Julianne blinked, clearly unhappy at being unpopular.

"God, this is so embarrassing!" Alder seethed.

Julianne managed a sweet but wounded smile. "Sorry, honey. They just needed my help."

By fifth hour, Alder was particularly cranky. The guys were giving her crap about how hot her mom was, and the girls were bugging her about why she was working as a substitute. Julianne had been a stay-at-home mom since a week before the three of us Erins were born. Before that she was a PA for Dr. Shuart's clinic, but she left Alder in daycare once and couldn't do it again. Or that was the story, anyway. Sam was Blackwell's general surgeon, and they lived in a six-bedroom home around the corner and down the street from Weston.

"What is that smell?" Sonny said loudly from the back of health class.

They had been on that subject all day, start-ing in first hour when Brady implied that the rancid chemical smell coming from some of Mrs. Merit's new supplies was coming from my vagina. After that, he made a show every time he passed me in the hall, and others caught on.

The thought of having them all in Health might have broken me, but for some reason, their taunts weren't fazing me like usual.

"Ugh," Brady said. "Again? What the hell is that? I've been smelling it all day!"

"Maybe it's you?" Weston said, turning around in his desk.

I kept facing forward.

Coach Morris turned from the chalkboard. "Is there a problem?"

Everyone shook their heads.

A muffled gagging noise came from the back, and then another. Coach turned around again.

"Sorry, Coach, but do you not smell that?" Sonny asked.

"No," he said, looking around, confused. "Smell what?" he sniffed, and everyone broke into laughter. The coach was not amused. "Either pay attention to the lesson or get out!" he shouted, pointing to the door. Everyone silenced.

"Yeah, dicks," Weston whispered.

Coach flipped around and his eyes targeted Weston. "What did you say, Gates?"

Weston swallowed. "I said, 'Yeah, dicks.'"

Coach Morris shifted his weight, preparing to lay into Weston. "And who are the dicks you're referring to?"

"That would be Brady, Sir, and anyone else complaining of a nonexistent smell."

Coach hesitated then turned back around.

"Fuck you, punk," Brady said under his breath.

"Suck my cock, Beck!" Weston said, standing up.

"All right, enough!" Coach Morris's voice boomed.

Mrs. Pyles walked in, her eyes wide. "Is everything okay in here?"

Coach glared at Brady and Weston. "Get out of my classroom. Both of you. Now."

Weston grabbed his backpack and stormed out.

Brady held up his hands. "I didn't do anything? Why are you throwing me out?"

"Get out, Brady!"

"But I didn't do anything! This is crap! Ask anyone!"

Coach Morris looked over at Mrs. Pyles. "Mrs. Pyles, would you please escort Mr. Beck out of my classroom before I lose my temper?"

Mrs. Pyles stared at him for a moment then walked toward Brady. "All right, Brady, let's go."

"Don't fucking touch me!" Brady said, his voice almost a whine.

"Brady Beck, get out of that chair, or so help me, I will assist Coach Morris in physically removing you from this classroom! Get up! Now!"

Brady leaned back against his seat as Mrs. Pyles leaned toward him. She was angrier than I'd ever seen her. After a moment of shock, Brady scrambled for his things and scurried from the classroom.

"You'll be hearing from my parents!"

"Oh, goody. Can't wait," Coach Morris deadpanned. "Now, back to the facial muscles."

I scooted down in my seat, feeling the ten pairs of eyes boring into the back of my head.

During seventh period, I kept glancing at Weston's empty seat and sighing. I didn't need him to save me, and it was causing him grief. I wasn't sure why he'd suddenly decided to take

43

me on as a cause, but it was clearly dangerous for both of us.

As I walked to the front of the school at the end of the day, I could see Brady, Brendan, Andrew, and the Erins standing on the corner that I usually crossed, next to their parallel-parked vehicles. Not once since they got their licenses had they congregated there, and I knew the Erins were already late for cheer practice. They were waiting for me.

I refused to take a different route to the Dairy Queen and lifted my chin as I approached, keeping my eyes forward.

"Hey," Sonny said. "We need to talk."

"I have nothing to say to you," I said, gripping the black, nylon straps of my backpack so tight my fingers hurt.

Alder smirked. "Maybe not, but we have a lot to say to you."

Brady grabbed my arm and flipped me around. "Don't be a fucking cunt. Let her speak."

I yanked my arm away, and just as the Erins were approaching me, a big, red truck pulled in next to us, the front tires climbing the curb with ease.

The driver's side door slammed, and Weston ran around the front, wedging his shoulder between Brady's hand and my arm.

"What are you doing, man?" Weston said.

Brady's expression turned severe. "What am I doing? What's wrong with you? Why are you busting my balls over this skank?"

"Just leave her alone, man," Weston said, trying to keep his voice calm.

"Weston," Alder said, reaching for his fingers. She looked like a beautiful, poisonous snake as she lithely crawled up Weston's side, rising on the balls of her feet. She kissed the corner of his mouth softly.

I had to fight a sudden bout of nausea.

Weston pulled away from her. "Go, Easter," he said quietly over his shoulder.

I turned on my heels and kept walking, refusing to look back. For the next five blocks, I tried to push the revolting image of Erin's toxic lips touching Weston. It was common knowledge that they were each other's firsts, but I tried not to think about it, and had successfully read all signs of oncoming PDA between the two for the last five years.

I slipped into the back door of the Dairy Queen, tying on my apron as I walked to the front.

"Hey chickiedoo! How was your day?" Frankie said, closing the window after her latest customer walked away.

"Weston got kicked out of class for taking up for me. The Erins and some of the guys were waiting for me after school."

"Aw! Wait…*what?*"

"You heard me," I said, crossing my arms and leaning my butt against the counter.

A minivan pulled into the parking lot, and several kids filed out. The mom came to my window, already looking worn. I took each of their orders, three of them changing while I was making them, and sent them on their way. After that, the lines formed and people kept adding to them until dark, so we didn't have much time to talk. When baseball practice let out, Weston's truck took off down Main Street, without stopping at the DQ. None of the players did..

We cleaned up, closed the shop, and walked outside. "Ride?" Frankie asked, but then stopped, mid-step.

Right outside the back door was Weston's red Chevy, towering over us. He was smiling down at me from the driver's seat. "Wanna take a drive?"

Frankie looked back at me, pleading with her eyes for me to say yes.

I nodded, and Weston disappeared, leaning over to pull the lever of the passenger door and pushing it open. I walked around the truck, but not without noticing Frankie's cheesy grin. I climbed up into the seat, and shut the door.

"I'm sorry about earlier," I said. "I just kind of left you there to deal with them alone."

"Stop. Don't you dare apologize to me."

When I didn't respond, he pulled the truck into gear and pulled away, down my street and past my house, straight out of town. I knew where we were going, and I was glad. It felt better than going home, or to school, or even the Dairy Queen. It had become the one place where I could relax and be at peace.

The Chevy's engine turned off, letting the silence of the night surround us. Weston opened the door and walked directly to the tailgate, pulling it down. This time he waited for me and held out his hand.

I stared at his fingers. They were long, and the nails had been bitten down to the quick. "I'm not…helpless."

"Oh, I know. I just think you're due for a little special treatment."

I looked at his outstretched hand.

He shrugged. "Just let me be nice to you."

I let him help me to the tailgate and watched as he climbed up and sat next to me.

"Oh," he said, leaning back and opening the cooler. He handed me a Fanta Orange, and he ended up with a Cherry Coke.

"Thank you," I said, taking a sip. "What did your parents say? About today?"

"They don't know."

"What do you mean? Didn't the school call them?"

"They didn't call Brady's, so they didn't call mine."

I sighed. "Well, I'm glad. I guess they didn't give you detention, either?"

"Nope."

I nodded. "Why did I even ask?"

He laughed once, without humor.

"When I got home, after practice, my dad had an acceptance letter in his hand. He was smiling from ear to ear. I wanted to puke."

"Why?"

"Because it was from his alma mater. Duke University. Don't get me wrong, it's a good school. My sister loves it there."

"Then what's the problem?"

"Another acceptance was in his other hand, from the Art Institute of Dallas." I waited while he took a sip of his Cherry Coke. "He didn't know I'd applied, and I tried to beat him home every day to check the mail so he wouldn't find out what I'd done."

"But today you didn't beat him, because you were standing on the corner with me."

"It's not your fault. He didn't even mention it. He didn't even care. He was too amped about the football scholarship, and even if I didn't get one, his mind was made up. It didn't even matter that I applied behind his back."

"What are you going to do?"

Weston pulled a wadded-up piece of paper from his letter jacket pocket. "I fished it out of the trash can."

I felt my eyes light up. "You're going to go?"

He stared at the paper. "I worked my ass off getting that application together."

"You're avoiding the question."

He looked at me. "What do you think? My parents won't help me with the tuition, much less an apartment."

"So you work and go to school. You're not the first student in the world to do that."

"I'm not scared of doing that. I'm just... that's a pretty big slap in the face to my parents. It's a big deal."

"It's your life." Those words were simple and overused, but that was always true of the truth. "What would your thirty-year-old self say?

"If he's sitting in an office pushing legal paperwork, he's probably cussing me."

I shrugged and looked up at the sky. "Sounds to me like you know the answer."

"It's a difference between want and should, isn't it?"

"Yes. You should do what you want."

He looked over at me and smiled, and I met his eyes. He watched me for a moment, and then his gaze fell to my lips. "You smell like ice cream."

My breath caught. "So?"

"I'm just kind of wondering if you taste like it."

After a short pause, I choked then burst out in howling laughter.

He grinned. "What? What's funny?"

I couldn't stop the ugly cackling bubbling up from deep inside of me, like it had been waiting there my entire life to be set free. My eyes watered. Weston quietly chuckled, too.

"Man," he said, rubbing the back of his neck. "I'm glad it's dark."

"Why's that?" I asked, wiping my eyes.

"Because my face has got to be bright red right now."

I nudged him. "Don't be embarrassed. Two weeks ago if someone told me you'd be saying that to me, I would have thought they were legitimately insane."

"Would you have wanted me to kiss you two weeks ago?"

I could only manage a side glance; then my line of sight dropped to my feet dangling from the tailgate. "No."

"No?"

"For the same reason I don't want you to kiss me now."

His eyes lit up with realization. "Alder."

"Yes," I said, pressing my lips into a hard line. He nodded once, conceding. "Is there something going on at the Diversion Dam tonight?" I asked, desperate to change the subject.

Weston leaned back and folded his arms behind his head. "I don't know, and I don't care."

I crawled up next to him, and while looking up at the stars, we exchanged memories about grade school, how much we loathed Mrs. Turner, and everything else in our world with the exception of Erin Alderman.

"Are you going to miss high school? I mean, you must," I said, shaking my head in amazement. "You're like a god here."

He laughed once; then his face crumbled. "The god of Hell is the devil. Not really much of a compliment."

"*Touché.*" I let my legs swing back and forth, feeling the chilly spring breeze blow through the thin fabric of my pants. It was warm enough that the bugs were chirping and buzzing in the grass. I listened to their symphony, our own little private show.

We drank our pops, and Weston crunched them in his man hands and tossed them behind us. He helped me down and walked around to my side, opening the door. I climbed up and sat, and he looked up at me.

"You doing anything for Spring Break?" he asked.

I shook my head.

"My parents are going skiing with our church group. I was supposed to go to South Padre with Alder and Brady and pretty much the whole football team and cheer squad, but I'm going to back out."

I frowned, confused.

Weston was clearly amused as he leaned his elbow on the bottom compartment of the door, looking up at me with his perfect, sweet smile. "I'm going to stay here."

"Won't your parents pitch a fit?"

"They'll understand. Besides, I'm eighteen. Not really much they can do."

"Alder won't understand."

"I'm not worried about it."

I narrowed my eyes. "You're going to leave me out of it, right?"

"Yes, Easter. I wouldn't throw you under the bus like that."

"I just feel like I should remind you that I'm moving away in a few months. I'm not crazy enough to think you're doing all of this for me, but if even a small part of it…"

"What if I was? Doing all of this for you."

"I would ask you why. Why all of a sudden are you so interested in me?"

"Who says it's all of a sudden?"

I tried not to smile. The only things that kept my face smooth were my next words, and I said them with conviction. "Weston, you're a nice guy. I'd be lying if I said I didn't like you. But I'm getting the hell out of here."

He shut the door and walked slowly to the driver's side. He stood at his door for a full minute. When he finally sat in his seat and switched on the ignition, he had to speak up over the roaring of the Chevy's glass packs. "So am I."

5.

"Can I talk to you for a minute? Like... not through this window?" Weston was pleading with his big emerald eyes. He'd been looking at me that way off and on for a week, in the hallway and in the classes we shared. I knew he wanted to say something to me, but things had been awkward between us since he dropped me off at my house several nights before.

I looked to Frankie. She pursed her lips and motioned for me to go to the back door.

"Yeah...yeah, you can uh...meet me in the back."

I turned on my heels and made my way to the back, every muscle in my body tense from my face to my toes. I pushed open the door, and Weston stepped inside. We stood alone in the storage room, with harsh fluorescent lighting making me look as horrible as possible, surrounded by boxes of syrup and toppings, and the weird smell from the drain wafting in the air. He didn't say anything at first, and my eyes drifted, targeting everything in the room except him, while I waited for him to speak.

"I'm a dick," he said, his eyebrows pulling in.

"What?"

"I'm worse than a dick. I'm a coward. I should have said something a long time ago. When you stood up to Erin, it just…gave me my balls back I guess. They're so damn mean, and I didn't want any of that directed at me, but…they're girls. They're teenage girls, and I'm ashamed that I've been too intimidated to say anything. Especially to Brady. What kind of asshole lets an asshole like that speak to a woman the way he speaks to you? I hated it. I've hated it for years, and I just tried to ignore it."

I shook my head. Brady, Brendan, and the Erins had said a few things to me that week, but nothing out of the ordinary. I wasn't sure what had Weston so riled up. "It's okay. I don't expect you to…"

"I know you don't. I've been thinking about this all week. All month. I'm not going to let them, or anyone else, treat you like that anymore." I wasn't sure what look I had on my face, but Weston suddenly seemed nervous. "What?"

"I don't know...I mean...you still haven't said why?"

He sighed. "I know. We're two months away from grad, and they've been torturing you since grade school. I can't go back, but I can make it up to you."

"That's it? That's your reason? You suddenly grew a conscience?"

He winced. "Ouch."

I crossed my arms. "Frankie has a long line out there, so let's get to the point. You're like a different person. You've turned against all of your friends and are hanging out with me, who you've barely spoken to since kindergarten. I think it's fair for me to ask why."

"I've talked to you as much as I could."

"As you *could*?"

He coughed into the crook of his arm. "That's not what I meant."

"I don't need you to save me, Weston. I've handled things on my own for a long time. I'm not a charity case."

He frowned. "I never said you were."

"We'd both probably be better off if you just returned to life as normal, and left me alone."

He winced, like my words had physically hurt him. "That's bullshit. You don't really feel that way, do you?"

"I don't know how I feel!"

"Neither do I!" he said, wheezing. He pulled his inhaler from his pocket and took a puff. After a few moments, he began again, this time calmer. "I don't know what I want to do with the rest of my life. And I feel like…I feel like you're the only person in the world that doesn't expect me to. What I do know is that I wasn't happy about the direction my life was going until you got into my truck that first night. I don't know what the hell I'm doing, Erin. I'm just…I'm winging it. I was kinda hoping you would wing it with me."

Despite every negative thought running through my head, my lips curved up.

He slowly pulled me against his chest and hugged me. His muscles were both soft and hard. My head fit perfectly beneath his chin. We stood like that for what seemed like a long while. He smelled like sweat, but the good kind of sweat. He could have smelled like the weird stuff that was fermenting in the floor drain, and I still would have liked it.

"I better get back up there," I said, my cheek still against his chest. He was a whole head taller than my five foot three inches, and I was glaringly aware of his fingers on my back, wrapping around to the side of my ribs. We had never been this close, even though I'd imagined what it must have felt like many times before.

He pulled away. "I'll see you later?"

"I have homework."

"Bring it with you."

I tucked my hair behind my ear. "I guess I can do that. If you leave me alone and let me finish."

"You won't even know I'm there."

He pushed through the door, and when it slammed behind him, I ran to the front, nearly smacking Frankie in the face with the swinging door.

Weston jogged to his truck, climbed in, and sped off, pausing for only a moment before pulling out onto Main Street.

Frankie watched me expectantly.

I shrugged.

"So he's your knight in shining armor, now?" she asked.

My face screwed up into disgust. "No. I told him I don't need to be saved. And you should already know that about me by now."

She smirked. "But it's kinda nice to be defended."

I tried not to smile, but lately it was impossible not to.

"I like him," Frankie said. "And so do you. But in a completely different way."

I made a face. "You have a vivid imagination."

"You're different since he started hangin' around."

"I don't know what you mean," I said, rolling my eyes and reaching for the closest rag.

"Well, you don't hate him."

I scrubbed the sink without actually paying attention to what I was doing. "Not today."

* * *

When we closed the Dairy Queen and walked out the back door, the red pickup wasn't parked in the back. It wasn't anywhere.

"I thought y'all had plans?" Frankie asked.

I shrugged.

"Ride?"

I shook my head and walked home. My hand touched the handle on our dirty screen door. I waited for the sound of his engine, but heard nothing. Soul Asylum drifted through the walls, and I was glad. If I was going to be stood up by Weston, I didn't want to have to deal with Gina, too.

I pushed through the door and headed straight back to my room. It felt lonelier than usual. A loud knocking came from the front door, and I rolled my eyes, assuming it was one of Gina's friends or her dealer, coming over to party. A few seconds later, Gina appeared in my doorway, her heavy mascara was smeared, the whites of her eyes bright red and glassy. She was still in her supermarket apron and her name badge was hanging crooked from her white polo shirt.

"It's for you." Her face mirrored my confusion.

I nodded and stood up, walking into the front room. I stopped in the middle of the carpet. Weston was standing in the front doorway, his hands in the pockets of his letterman jacket. The body of the coat was maroon-dyed wool, and a big Chenille B was stitched to the left side, outlined in white. Weston's jacket was almost too busy with everything he'd lettered in during his high school career, especially with the numerous patches on his leather sleeves. I'd never wanted a letterman, and it was weird to see someone wearing one in my living room.

Gina stood next to me, gawking at him. She scratched her arm and nodded toward him. "Who is he?"

Weston held out his hand. "Weston Gates, ma'am. I'm a friend of Erin's."

Gina hesitated, but she finally shook his hand then looked to me. "Are you going somewhere?"

I nodded.

"Erin was going to help me with my homework." He lied seamlessly, as if he'd done it a thousand times before.

"Oh," Gina said, satisfied. That probably made sense to her, because she couldn't fathom someone like Weston Gates wanting anything else from me.

I rushed to my room to change and gathered my things. A minute later, I was behind Weston, hurrying him outside. Once we got into his truck, I sighed. "I wish you wouldn't have done that. I didn't want you to see my house."

"Why not?"

"It's filthy. It smells."

"All I smelled was weed. Your mom is baked," he said, amused. When he realized I wasn't, he reached over for my forearm. "Hey. It's a house, Erin. It's not a big deal. I don't care where you live."

"It's just humiliating," I said, wiping a tear away. "I didn't want you to see that."

Weston pulled away from the curb, his jaw working under his skin. "I didn't mean to make you cry, Erin, I'm sorry. I thought it was nicer than picking you up from the DQ. I thought I'd introduce myself to your mom."

"She's not my mom," I said staring out the window.

"Huh?"

"Her name is Gina."

"Are you adopted?"

"No. But," I looked over at him, "do you ever get the feeling that you belong somewhere else?"

"All the time," he said, sounding exhausted.

"I've never felt like her daughter. Not even when I was little."

"Maybe it's because she's the way she is? She doesn't seem like the mom type."

"She's not."

"Then it makes sense that you would feel that way."

We weren't driving out of town like we usually did. Instead, we were driving to the south side, where many of the doctors and attorneys lived. Weston's parents built a huge house on a lot there when we were in middle school. He pulled into his driveway and under the arch that attached the house to one of the garages. The spot was enclosed by garage doors, the side of the house, and a gate to the backyard.

When he turned off the engine, I shook my head. "I'm not going in there."

"Oh, quit it," Weston said, pressing the garage door opener. Hopping down, he slammed his door and then jogged around to my side, opening my door with a wide grin. When I didn't budge, his face fell. "Don't be such a baby."

I slowly climbed down and followed him into the garage and through a door. The house was dark, but a television was on somewhere. The dim blue light grew brighter as we approached the kitchen.

"Weston?" a woman called.

"I'm home, Mom!" he called back. He slipped my backpack off my shoulders and set it on the counter.

"Weston, what are you doing?" I said through my teeth, getting angrier by the second.

His mother walked into the kitchen, her highlighted hair and oval face accentuating her amazing green eyes. It was clear who Weston favored. She stopped, surprised to see me. I wanted to crawl under the counter.

"Who's this?" she said, with fake cheerfulness in her voice.

"Erin Easter." He looked at me. "This is my mom, Veronica."

"Nice to meet you," I choked out.

She gave me a once over, visibly unimpressed with my appearance. Her eyes critically assessed me like I was a parasite that had infiltrated her home and needed to be exterminated. Weston didn't seem to notice. He opened the pantry, grabbed a bag of chips, a jar of salsa, and two bananas then pulled a couple of cold cans of Cherry Coke from the fridge.

"We're going downstairs," he said.

"Weston Allen," Veronica began.

"Night, Mom," he said, guiding me in front of him toward a door down the hall. I grabbed my backpack and walked slowly, unsure of where to go.

"This one," Weston said.

I opened it, and he walked past, using his elbow to flip on the light, revealing a flight of stairs leading to a lower level. When we reached the bottom, we walked into a vast room with couches, a couple of televisions, a gaming system, a wet bar, exercise equipment, a pool table, and an air hockey table.

That one room was bigger than my entire house.

"Whoa," I said quietly, letting Weston lead me to the couch.

"This is my space. They won't bug us down here." He unscrewed the lid of the salsa, and the bag of tortilla chips crackled as he unrolled it. "You hungry?"

"I'll take that banana," I said, pointing.

He tossed it to me. "I'll wait."

"For what?"

"Until you finish your homework. I'm going to find us a movie to watch."

I watched him while he pushed buttons on the remote without looking at them, turning on the DVR and browsing the movies on demand. I pulled out my textbook. A piece of notebook paper stuck out from the page I needed, and I worked on the nine questions I had left to answer. It took only about fifteen minutes to finish, and Weston remained quiet, keeping his word.

Once I closed my book and packed away my things, he excitedly returned his focus to me. "Do you want to watch *Triple Thunder*, or *The Dark House on the Hill*?"

"Both sound equally…entertaining."

"*Triple Thunder* it is." He pushed a button on the remote, and the screen turned black for a moment. He chose a few more options; then the movie began, opening with a sweaty guy running for his life in a desert.

Halfway through the movie, Weston leaned back against the couch cushion, his size twelves crossed at the ankle on top of the ottoman that doubled as a coffee table. I had a more difficult time relaxing.

Weston looked over at me, back at the television, and then back at me.

"What?"

"You're so uptight. Do you want me to take you home?"

"I just...I don't think your mom likes that I'm here. And I..."

Weston's phone chirped. Alder's name lit up the display. He read the text in less than a second, then shot one back.

"What if your mom mentions to Alder that I was here?"

"She won't."

"How can you be sure?"

"She doesn't want Alder to be mad at me. She's already envisioning Gates-Alderman grandchildren."

My face screwed into disgust. "You should probably take me home."

He sat up. "Why? You don't like the movie?"

"It's not okay for me to be here. You have a girlfriend, and we're..."

"Sneaking around?" Weston said with a sweet grin. "Fine." He picked up his phone.

"What are you doing?" I asked while he tapped out a message.

"Breaking up with Alder."

6.

I GRABBED HIS PHONE AND HELD it away from him. "Are you trying to make things worse?"

"No. But you telling me you won't hang out with me because of a girl I don't even like anymore...that's an easy fix."

"Why would you stay with someone you don't like for five years?"

He shrugged. "Something to do, I guess. She's not ugly."

"No," I said, sighing. "She's not. You sound like a huge asshole right now."

"Do we have to talk about this?"

"No, you can just take me home."

He groaned, and then sat up, facing me. "My parents have been married for twenty years, and they don't really like each other." He paused, and when he realized I wasn't satisfied, he continued, "I liked her at first, but I never liked the way she treated people. You, in particular. When I talked to her about you, she just seemed to treat you worse. But every time I thought about breaking it off with her, the drama I knew would follow didn't sound all that appealing."

"Five years is a long time," I said.

"You have no idea."

"So are you just going to wait until you leave for college?"

"That was the plan, but now I kind of want to do it sooner." He leaned toward me, and I leaned away. He snorted. "You're really going to make me do this by the book, aren't you?"

"I'm not making you do anything," I said, handing him back his phone.

"You're making me miss this movie."

I glanced at the television. "It's paused."

"Oh, yeah," he said with a smile, pushing a button. The violence ensued, along with screaming, gun shots, and helicopter blades whirring in the air. Weston settled back into the cushions again, and I did the same.

He looked down at his phone, still in his hand. "What's your number, anyway?"

"I don't have a cell phone."

"Landline?"

"Nope."

Weston frowned, but kept his eyes on the television screen. "Do you like hanging out with me?"

I wasn't sure if I'd heard him right. "Yes?"

"Not because you don't have anyone else to hang out with?"

"I have other people to hang out with."

"Frankie?"

"Yes."

"What if I wasn't with Alder? Would you…?" He stared at the TV.

"Would I what?"

"Let me kiss you?"

"I don't know. Maybe. I'm not sure you'd enjoy it."

He turned to me. "What makes you say that?"

"I haven't had a lot of practice. None, actually." I could feel my face heat up. I preferred to tell the truth, but it wasn't always easy.

"You've never kissed anyone before," he said, as more of a statement than a question.

"So?"

He stared at my lips and readjusted so he could look straight ahead again. "I'm available whenever. If you want to practice." He was purposefully keeping his face smooth, but he wasn't doing a very good job because the corner of his mouth kept trying to curl up.

"I don't want to practice. I want a real first kiss. And not from a guy who's cheating on his girlfriend."

He frowned. "I told you I'd break up with her. You don't want me to."

"We'd never have a moment of peace. The whole school would freak out, and I'm pretty sure your mom would, too."

"Is that why you don't want me to break up with her? Or is it because you just don't want me?"

I kept quiet, and the air in the room became thick and stuffy. It was suddenly hard to breathe. Weston squirmed while he waited for my answer.

"I've thought you were kind of amazing since kindergarten," I said.

He peeked over at me and grinned. "Yeah?"

"Yeah."

With his eyes back on the television, he spoke softly and nervously. "Me, too. About you."

I nodded, and we watched the rest of the movie without another word.

When it was over, Weston put on his jacket, picked up my backpack, and walked me upstairs. He snatched his keys from the kitchen counter. We made our way outside into the chilly night air. Weston pulled off his jacket and draped it over my shoulders. It was warm and smelled like him, and I pulled it tighter around me. Weston helped me climb into the passenger seat. Before he could round the front of the truck, his parents came outside to talk to him.

Their conversation immediately looked tense, and Weston kept stealing glances at me. He put his hands on his hips, shifted his weight nervously, and shook his head a lot. He was beginning to look angry. I wished he didn't have automatic windows so I could roll mine down to hear what they were saying.

Finally, his parents turned to go inside, and Weston joined me in the truck.

"Sorry about that," he said.

"Don't be."

"No, that's just fucking rude to do that in front of you. They could have waited."

"What did they say?"

He shook his head and backed out of the drive. When he pulled onto the street, I reached over and touched my fingertips to his. He intertwined his fingers in mine.

jamie mcguire

"What did they say, Weston?"

He sighed. "They're concerned about my new friend. They don't think it's appropriate for me to be spending time alone with you because of Alder."

"They're right."

He squeezed my fingers. "I can't give you up now. When we spend time together, I feel this peace that I don't get when you're not around. It's kind of like when you're a kid, and you put on fresh PJs after a bath and get into a made bed with clean sheets straight out of the dryer. That's what being with you feels like."

My eyebrows lifted, and a surprised, appreciative smile swept across my face. "I think that's the nicest thing anyone's ever said to me."

"It shouldn't be. You're so good, Erin. You're just…good. You don't deserve the way they treat you, and I don't even know why they do it."

"I don't know, either. One day, they just stopped talking to me, and then the silence turned into anger."

"That's so weird. I don't get it."

The Chevy pulled into my gravel drive, and Weston put the gear into park.

74

I leaned back and stretched. "Just one more day before Spring Break. After that we have five weeks before graduation. None of this will matter after that."

"Are you…are you going to prom?" he asked.

I laughed once. It was shrill, and it even surprised me. "No," I said, amused.

"Would you want to go with me?"

"You're going with Alder."

"I haven't asked her, yet. Everyone just assumes we're going together. Even her."

"I…" I shook my head, feeling over-whelmed. "I don't have a dress. I wouldn't even know where to look. And I don't have the money, anyway."

"Okay. Don't freak out. Just think about it. If you want to go, we'll figure something out."

I swallowed, hard. "You're freaking me out. I'm not sure how to feel about all of this."

Weston lifted my hand and touched his lips to my fingers. "We're just winging it, remember?"

I pulled the door handle and jumped down to the grass below, then pulled his jacket from my shoulders.

"Hang on to it for me."

I tossed it into his truck. "I have a jacket. Thank you."

He smirked. "Not one that smells like me."

"Are you afraid I'm going to forget about you overnight?" I teased, trying to hide my embarrassment that he'd spoken my private thought.

He pointed to his chest. "This? No way!"

Weston waved to me as he pulled away, and I walked into my house, still giggling. It was dark and quiet. I crept into my room and let my backpack fall to the carpet, and crawled straight into bed. I was too tired to take a shower or even brush my teeth. I just wanted to lie between the sheets and replay what Weston said about how I made him feel over and over again in my head. It was like a dream, one that I would inevitably wake up from soon. Something was going to come along and take it all away, because things like this didn't happen to me.

I reached over and set my alarm for half an hour earlier than usual, and then relaxed against my pillow. Tomorrow was Friday, the last day before Spring Break, and the beginning of a week-long vacation from the Erins, and nine whole days and evenings with Weston, doing whatever we wanted. He was becoming my best friend, and not just because he was my only friend at school. We actually had a lot in common, from music to art to a mutual love for the first three episodes of *Star Wars*.

I felt my eyes grow heavy, and I drifted off, with his words about PJs and warm sheets playing over in my mind, narrated by his smooth, deep voice.

7.

FRIDAY MORNING, I STEPPED out of my home to see a white SUV parallel parked next to the curb. Mrs. Pyles rolled down the window and waved.

"I told you I would be here!" she called, a big grin on her face.

I looked up. The clouds were gray, the sidewalk and grass were wet, but the raining had stopped. "I think it's okay to walk."

"It's supposed to rain on and off all day, Easter. Get your rear in this car!"

I turned around, double-checking that Gina wasn't watching me from the door then hurried to Mrs. Pyles's vehicle.

"Buckle up," she said, twisting the key in the ignition.

"Can we please hurry?" I asked, hearing the click at my hip as I fastened the seat belt.

She pulled away, and moments later, paused at a stop sign. A blue pickup passed through the puddle that always filled the corner of that intersection when it rained, splashing water all the way up the sign.

"If you'd been standing there, you would have been soaked," Mrs. Pyles said, shaking her head.

"Thank you," I said, biting at my thumbnail.

She pulled forward, and after a block, stopped at another stop sign. I looked over at the Dairy Queen. It was dark and the parking lot was bare. If it kept raining, we wouldn't be much busier after school. Just as that thought crossed my mind, the sky began spitting on us.

Mrs. Pyles turned right toward the school, her blond hair grazing her shoulders as she leaned forward to turn on the windshield wipers. "Do you have plans for Spring Break?" she asked.

"Not really."

"You're not going to South Padre with the other seniors?" I gave her a side look. She smiled sheepishly. "I've noticed you've been spending time with Weston Gates. I thought maybe you would. Hoped maybe you would."

"You've noticed?" I said, my heart beating fast. I thought we were being careful. Weston had been taking up for me in class, but I thought no one knew that we'd actually been spending time together.

She smiled her sweet smile. "Veronica Gates is in my women's auxiliary church group. She's talked about you two a little bit lately. That's all. Just to me."

"She doesn't want anyone else to know, I'm sure."

"She doesn't want to cause problems."

"For Weston and Alder."

We parked in the teacher's lot, and Mrs. Pyles turned to me. "He's a nice boy."

I waited, imagining she might tell me to stay away from him, or something equally offensive.

"You sure can pick 'em," she said, winking at me.

She got out and shut her door. After briefly processing her words and feeling half a second of appreciation, I got out and hurried to walk next to her. We strode toward the school, dry under Mrs. Pyles's umbrella. She pointed her key ring at the white SUV, and it made a stunted honking noise as it locked.

In grade school, before I realized I wouldn't get a car at sixteen, I dreamed about what car I wanted. No matter what it was, it always had keyless entry. Something about holding that remote in my hand while the keys dangled from it seemed so cool. Then sixteen came and went, and so did seventeen. I went ahead and got my license, just to have an ID, but there was no point. Owning a car seemed so impossible. So I would just do one impossible thing at a time, starting with somehow getting myself to OSU's campus. But even if I had to start walking in July, I would get there. Maybe, if he wasn't already at Dallas or Duke, Weston could drop me off.

That thought warmed me as I walked down the long hallway lined with lockers, across the commons area to a set that sat alone in the middle of the floor next to the library. I specifically requested a locker here because, even though it wasn't with the rest of the seniors, the library was surrounded by a wall of glass, and the librarian, Mrs. Boesch, always kept a watchful eye between classes.

I pulled books out of my backpack and hung it up on a hook. The morning sun streaming in through the front windows of the school was suddenly blocked, and I looked to my right to see Weston leaning against the locker next to mine.

"What are you doing after work tonight?"

I shrugged.

"Let's eat at Los Potros."

I looked around, and then nodded.

Weston beamed and walked away, not trying the slightest bit to conceal our conversation. I shut my locker, and Sara Glenn stared at me with her big, dark eyes.

"Are you screwing Weston Gates?" she asked.

I narrowed my eyes at her, disgust weighing down my face. What was it with small-town people automatically assuming that because two people of the opposite sex were speaking, they must be having sex? "No."

"What was that, then? He just asked you to dinner. Why is he asking you out?"

"He didn't ask me to dinner. You heard him wrong," I said. Technically, it was the truth. He didn't ask.

"I heard him," Sara snapped. "I'm telling Alder."

"Go ahead. She won't believe you. She'll assume you're trying to get them to break up so you can take a stab at him."

Sara thought about that for a moment, and then walked away, her confidence gone.

I took a deep breath and continued to class, my hands shaking and my heart trying to beat its way out of my chest. That sudden burst of courage came from deep inside; a place I didn't know existed. The thought of Sara ruining my little bit of happiness made me desperate enough to offer a threat that I myself found frightening.

Everyone was too excited about South Padre to bother giving me grief. By the time I'd made it to seventh period, as weird as it was to say, I'd actually had a pretty good day. Weston had pulled his stool over to my desk, and a combination of nausea and exhilaration swirled in my stomach.

"Check this out," Weston said. His poster-sized project was spread out across the table, and I looked it over with an uncontrollable smile. It was a girl looking out the window, her face in shadow except for her bright blue eyes. She held her knees to her chest, and a small necklace hung loosely from her fingers. It was a silver heart with intricate detail chiseled around the border. In the middle appeared one word: Happenstance.

"It's incredible," I whispered. "She's so pretty." I felt an urge to run my fingers over it, but didn't want to smear the charcoal.

"It's you."

I looked up at him, in shock. We'd been working on this project for three months. My eyebrow shot up, and I shook my head, unconvinced. "You're such a liar."

"I'm completely serious."

"Is everyone ready to reveal their final project?" Mrs. Cup said as she sauntered into the classroom, dressed in a black shawl and pants suit. "I know you have all been working incredibly hard. In years past, you've taken home these projects and framed them, given them away, or did with them as you choose. But I've asked more from you this year. We've learned about Faulkner's lessons and that as artists, you must learn to kill your darlings." She sighed. "For your final grade, I'm going to ask this of you." She held up Shannon LaBlue's poster-sized painting and ripped it in half, length-wise. It made a quick, high-pitched sound, and we all gasped.

Shannon's mouth fell open. She looked around, unsure of what to do.

Mrs. Cup walked to Zach Skidmore, who sat next to me. "Well?"

"Are you serious? I thought this was going to be the crowning project of my high school years. I worked my ass off on this, Mrs. Cup!"

"It's your final grade."

Zach stared at the ground for a moment, breathed out through his nose, and then took his project, a beautiful landscape, and ripped it in half. We all winced, as if he'd cut his wrists.

The teacher stood in front of my desk. I had worked hard on my project, a charcoal piece featuring a dark hallway with Victorian paintings. It made a horrid ripping sound as I separated one side from the other.

Mrs. Cup took a step, standing in front of Weston. His project was still laid out on my desk, behind him.

"Weston."

"This is cruel," he said.

"It's a lesson. Not all lessons are easy. The best ones—those you learn the most from—are the most difficult."

"I'm not doing it," Weston said, shifting just slightly, protecting his elegant and tender rendering of me.

"It's your final grade, Weston. It was the whole point."

He stood, pulled his poster from the desk, and rolled it carefully. "Then I guess I fail." He left the classroom and walked down the hall toward the parking lot.

Mrs. Cup shook her head, then took a step toward the next horrified student.

"It was you?" Frankie asked, a little stunned.

I nodded.

"An art project he'd been working on for three months...and it was you?"

"It was me."

"Whoa. And he failed his art class to keep it. That's...that's kind of poignant."

"I kind of thought that, but I wasn't sure if I was reading it wrong."

"How can you read that wrong? It's so romantic I could die!" She bent over, nearly in half, pretending to sob in a very unflattering way.

"That's ugly," I said, trying to stifle a grin.

"It's soooo beautiful! I can't stand it! Agh ha ha!"

"Stop," I said, scooping M&Ms into the cup of vanilla I'd just pulled out.

She stood up. "Sorry. I had a moment."

I handed the M&M Blizzard to the little girl. She turned on her heels, revealing my next customer, Alder. Her eyes were red, and she was beyond pissed.

"What are you doing?" she asked, her voice already breaking.

"We were just joking around. What can I get you?" I asked.

"Fuck you. You know what I'm talking about, Easter," she seethed.

My mind raced for a response, but she hadn't come for a fight. She was alone, and that wasn't like the Erins.

She cocked her head a bit, impatient with my silence. "Answer me. And don't you dare pretend to be innocent. We both know what's been going on."

Frankie stood beside me. "She's working, Alder. You can talk about this later."

"No, I can't," she said, her eyes glossing over. "Because I'm leaving in half an hour for South Padre. I was supposed to be riding with Weston, but he's suddenly decided that he doesn't want to go, so I'm riding with Sonny. Explain to me why that is, Easter."

"I can't speak for him."

"Well someone's going to have to. The only thing he said was that it wasn't working out between us."

"He broke up with you?"

Alder put both of her hands on the little counter in front of the window, palms down. "That's what you wanted, isn't it?"

"I never expected him to," I said. It was the truth.

"He didn't have a lot of time to go into details, because he was taking some stupid drawing to Ponca City to have it framed."

I choked. "He…what?"

"So you can tell me, Easter. Why are you doing this to me?"

"I'm sorry," I said, that same anger I felt with Sara bubbling up again. "Why am *I* doing something to *you*?"

"Has he been cheating on me? I deserve to know!"

Frankie put her hand on her hip. "If he broke up with you, does it really matter?"

Alder's eyes targeted Frankie. "Oh, go push out another kid, Frankie."

Frankie slowly moved me to the side and leaned down. "You need to leave right now, or you're going to have to try to enjoy your senior trip with no boyfriend and a new black eye. Because I will come through this window at you."

Alder rolled her eyes. She walked away, but stopped and came back. "You watch yourself,

Easter. When I get back, I'm going to make it my mission to make you so miserable you'll have to finish high school at home. You think I've been mean to you? You haven't seen anything yet."

"That sounds like a threat." Frankie narrowed her eyes at Alder.

Alder smiled, but she looked more frightening that I've ever seen her. "I don't make threats. I'm just giving her an idea of what the next six weeks of her life are going to be like."

"Same thing," Frankie said.

"I'm going to go enjoy my Spring Break. You should really try to enjoy yours."

"I will," I said, lifting my chin.

She shot me a look that made my blood run cold and returned to her Honda.

"Whew! You lit a fire under her ass!" Frankie said, nearly euphoric from the confrontation.

I leaned my butt against the counter. "She's serious. When she gets back, it's going to be hell."

"Who cares?" Frankie said with a wink. "You've got Weston."

"I don't *have* him."

"He's framing your drawing." She sighed. "He's got it bad."

"This is all really weird. Everything has been the same every day since first grade. Things have steadily gotten worse, and now they're...I don't know."

"Amazing?"

"Different."

Frankie nodded. An SUV pulled into the parking lot, and four kids hopped out, followed by their toddler-toting mother. Frankie and I got back to work.

I was feeling even more excited for Spring Break. If I was going to be punished for it, I was going to make sure every second was worth it.

8.

WESTON'S TRUCK WAS PARKED directly behind the Dairy Queen. As if he already didn't look happy enough, I brought him an extra tall Cherry Dip Cone. His grin spread from ear to ear.

"Do I have time to go home and change?" I asked.

"Nope. I'm too excited to show you something."

We drove to his house. The windows were dark, and when he pressed the garage door button, his parents' vehicle wasn't in its spot. Even though it was a weekend, the entire town seemed to be closed down. With all the upperclassman traffic gone during Spring Break and so many families away for vacation, Blackwell would be on a week-long sleep; it was that way every year.

"Your parents already left?" I asked.

He nodded. "This morning."

"What did they say about you staying home?"

He held open the door for me, and I walked through to the hallway. "It was a little weird. They were confused, and Mom's freaking out about Alder, but they also seemed relieved. I think they were letting me go because I'm eighteen, but they were going to be worried about me the whole time."

"Makes sense."

"They asked me if I wanted to go skiing, but it's their first adults-only vacation since they had me, so they were kind of glad I said no."

I chuckled. His life was so fascinating to me. The way he was so close with his parents, how they understood each other and cared for each other was foreign to me. But mostly I liked that they were sober and could solve their issues without yelling at him.

We went to the main stairs, and Weston flipped on the light. I followed him up the spiral, wooden staircase. There was a polished wooden banister with intricate iron instead of spindles. I loved his house. It was so clean, and decorated with such care that it could have been featured in a home design magazine.

Hanging from the clay-colored wall were canvases of Weston and his older sister Whitney, posing together and individually, from grade school to senior year.

When we reached the top of the stairs, Weston walked down another hallway, and then opened the last door on the left, sweeping his arm across his body, signaling for me to come in. The room was still dark, but when I stepped inside, Weston flipped on the light, revealing his bed, a dresser, and a desk. Like the rest of the house, everything had its place. It was all dusted and smelled fresh. The midnight blue comforter was tucked under the pillows, and smoothed out just right. The desk was organized and dusted, and his brand new computer was off.

Above the desk was the charcoal he'd drawn of me. Its frame was black and looked like rope. It didn't really go with the brown stained wooden frame of his bed, or anything else in his room.

"What do you think?"

I realized then that my mouth was open and I snapped it shut.

His eyebrows pulled together. "I went to Hobby Lobby in Ponca to get it framed. It wasn't the frame I wanted, but they would have had to order the other one, and I wanted to show it to you today. I couldn't wait."

"Are you really going to fail Art?"

He shrugged. "Who cares? What do you think?"

"The Art Institute of Dallas might take issue with you failing Art."

His shoulders fell. "I'm not going to Dallas, Erin."

"Why not?"

"I tried to tell my parents, but I can't look them in the eye and say it to them."

"Do you want to go?"

He held out his hands then let them fall back to his thighs with a slap. "Yeah."

"Then you're going. We're going to figure out a way to get you there, even if I have to hold your hand when you tell them. They love you, Weston, and above all, they want you to be happy, right?"

He nodded slowly. "But…"

"No buts. We're going to get you there."

He watched me for a moment. "Do you like the frame?"

"I love the frame. I love the picture. I still don't understand why you decided to make me your final project." My last words hung in the air. "Is that what I am? A project?"

He seemed disappointed by my question. "I didn't know what I was going to do. I just started drawing. After a week I realized that she," he said, pointing to the drawing, "was you. As I put more time into making her perfect, I understood why it happened." He took a few steps toward me, until he was so close I had to look up to see his eyes. "When you think about something enough, you start dreaming about it. And when you dream about something enough, you just have to hope that it becomes a reality." He sighed. "I think about you all the time, Erin. I've wanted to talk to you for years, but I was just so damn nervous. I didn't know what to say or how you'd react if I did. I was afraid you would think I was just trying to help Alder pick on you. I know that I have shitty timing, because we're both getting ready to move in different directions, but I've gotten really good at loving you from a distance."

I'd worked so hard not to let anyone see me cry that I felt a moment of panic when my eyes watered and the first tear fell. I quickly wiped it away.

Weston put his thumbs on each side of my face and leaned down, pausing just before he whispered, "Can I kiss you?"

I nodded slowly, feeling every nerve in my body perk up and wait to experience what was about to happen.

Weston leaned in, closed his eyes, and pressed his lips to mine. They were so soft and warm. His lips parted, so I did the same. I'd seen kissing on television enough to know how this worked, so I just tried to keep my lips soft and moved with him. His tongue slipped into my mouth and danced with mine. He tasted like Cherry Dip Cone and toothpaste, which was oddly fantastic. His hands slid down from my jaw to my neck, and then to my shoulders. His fingers pressed into my skin as he pulled me gently closer.

Just when I thought I was going to pass out from holding my breath, I heard Weston breathe slightly through his nose, and I did the same. I was completely clueless, so I just kept taking cues from him.

He pulled away, and I nearly fell forward because I wasn't ready to stop yet.

"Whoa," he said, staring at me.

"What? Was it awful?"

He shook his head. "No. Not at all. But we'd better stop." He sat on the bed and took a deep breath, rubbing the back of his head. He stared at the floor. "Just…give me a minute."

I walked over to him and crashed against his chest. His back slammed against the bed, and I put my mouth on his. He wrapped his arms around me and hugged me to him, making a low humming noise as our tongues found their way to each other again. We grabbed at each other, barely coming up for air, and at one point or another over the next hour, we occupied every inch of his queen-sized bed.

Finally, Weston let his head fall back to his pillow, keeping his arms wrapped tightly around me. I was halfway on top of him, lying on my side, my leg draped over one of his. "I'm going to be hurting in the morning already. We have to stop."

"Why will you be hurting?"

He paused, clearly trying to search for gentle words to explain. "I feel like an ass explaining. It'll make it sound like I'm trying to guilt trip you into…you know. And it was never my intention for you to experience your first kiss and lose your virginity in the same night."

"Are we talking about blue balls?"

He choked then busted out into loud laughter. Once he caught his breath, he pulled my fingers up to his mouth and kissed them. "Yes."

"I'm not completely clueless. I am aware of most things, even if I haven't experienced them for myself."

"Something you might not be aware of is that I'm not cheating on Alder. I broke up with her today."

"I know."

He readjusted his head on the pillow to look straight at me. "How?"

"She came by the DQ today. She was pretty upset."

"Was she mean to you?" he said. His jaws worked under the skin as he waited for me to answer.

"She's always mean to me. But she said when she gets back that it's going to get significantly worse."

Weston looked away, and then back at me. "I won't let them hurt you anymore, Erin. Don't be afraid of them."

"I'm not."

He frowned. "It's just six weeks. We can get through it."

I kissed him, this time it was brief and sweet. Just a peck, then I nodded. "You're the one I'm worried about. You're not used to it."

"I'm happier than I've been in a long time. They might give us shit during school, but they can't touch what we've got."

I rested my head on his chest and listened to his heart beating. It slowed more with each passing minute, and then his breathing became deep and even. I glanced up, seeing that his eyes were closed. His hand was resting comfortably on my back. I laid my head back down, nestling against his side and snuggling into his neck. He pulled me closer to him, and that is when I fell asleep.

* * *

At first, the chirping didn't register, but when Weston tried to carefully maneuver out from under me, I woke up.

"Sorry," he whispered. "It's four in the morning. Go back to sleep."

"What's going on?" I asked, wiping my eyes.

"I don't know. Someone is blowing up my phone." Right when he reached for his cell and unplugged it from the charger, it rang. "Shit, it's my Mom. Hello?"

I could hear Veronica on the other end, her voice high-pitched and desperate.

"No. Calm down, Mom. No, I told you. I'm in Blackwell. I stayed here, remember? Mom. Stop crying. What's going on?"

The voice switched to a deep tone, and I could tell it was Peter, Weston's father. Weston wiped his face, his eyes were wide.

"Holy shit. Are you sure? Who told you?" He paused, listening to Peter. "Oh, man. Both of them? I don't…Jesus. No, don't come back. I'm fine. No, I'm sure. You guys try to have a good time. I'm at home, safe in my bed. Okay. Love you, too." He hung up the phone and looked down at me.

"What is it? Are they okay?"

"Yeah, they're fine. It's the Erins. They were on their way to South Padre, and Alder was driving. She fell asleep or something and crossed the median. They hit a semi head on. They're dead."

"They're…*dead*?" I said in disbelief.

Weston wiped his face again and held his hand over his mouth. "They're dead. Sonny and Alder are dead." His eyes were wide, and my mouth hung open. We sat in silence for the longest time.

Weston grabbed his phone and checked his messages. He sighed and shook his head. "The rumors are already starting." He put down the phone. "Should I take you home?"

"Whatever you want to do. If you want to be alone, I can walk home. If you don't, I'll stay here."

He pulled me against him and leaned back against the pillows, but we didn't sleep.

9.

THE FUNERALS WERE HELD together the following Saturday. I didn't go, because it didn't feel right, but Weston stopped by the Dairy Queen afterward to fill me in. He told me Sonny's parents and Sam and Julianne seemed to be holding up well and leaned on each other for support. He talked about what the funeral looked like, who ran the service, what songs they played and who was there. But he seemed lost.

"Why don't you go?" Frankie said. "He needs you today."

"I..." I looked to Weston. "Do you want me to take off?"

He looked pitiful. "Please?"

I pulled off my apron and tossed it on the counter. "Thanks, Frankie."

She winked at me, but her expression was sad.

I pushed through the back door, and went immediately into Weston's arms. He held me tight, burying his head in my neck. I held him for a long time, but when I pulled away, he hung on, so I kept my arms around him, squeezing tighter.

Once his arms relaxed, he handed me his keys. "Would you drive?"

I froze. "I've only driven the Driver's Ed car, and that was over two years ago."

"You can do it," he said. He opened the door and helped me into the driver's seat; then he jogged around and climbed in next to me.

I nervously turned the key in the ignition, adjusted the seat and mirrors, all while trying to recall everything I learned about driving. I pressed on the brake and then pulled the gear into drive, pulling forward. I paused at Main Street before driving out of the parking lot. "Where do you want to go?"

"Anywhere. Just drive." He reached over and took my hand into his. As I turned right and headed out of town, Weston rested his head against the seat. "Everyone was apologizing to me today. It felt so weird, because I don't feel like I lost anything. I should feel different. Is it weird that I don't?"

"I don't know how to feel either. I try not to think about it."

"Maybe it's not acceptable, or maybe others wouldn't understand." He turned to look at me. "But we get it. We can talk about it to each other."

I waited for him to expand on that thought. The Erins couldn't make good on Alder's promise to make me miserable, now, and that was a good thing. But I didn't want to be the first one to say something so appalling out loud.

He looked up. "I'm sorry they were hurt. I'm sorry they lost their lives, but I feel sort of...relieved. It feels like such an asshole thing to say, but it's the truth. Don't you feel the same?"

"I'm not glad they're dead." I took a deep breath. "But it's a relief to know they can't torture me anymore."

Weston squeezed my hand, and after that. We didn't talk much. I drove until the gas light lit up on the dash. By then we were an hour south, in Stillwater. Weston directed me to the nearest gas station and showed me how to pump the gas.

"You hungry?" he asked.

"A little."

"Okay, I'll grab some chips and a pizza pocket or something. Mountain Dew?"

I nodded. "Thank you."

He hung the nozzle on the pump, and then ran into the station. I stood there, not sure which door to get in. When Weston returned, he watched me, puzzled.

"What are you doing, babe?"

My purpose, where I was, and even my own name were lost on me, because of what had just come out of his mouth. I'd heard other couples call each other sweet terms of endearment, and I heard mothers say such things to their children, but no one had called me anything but my name, and a few colorful slurs. I'd always imagined what it would feel like, to hear someone who loved me call me something simple and sweet, and it just came out of Weston Gates's mouth.

I tried to speak, but nothing came out.

"Do you want me to drive?" he asked. When I didn't respond, he took another step toward me. "Are you okay?"

I took a few quick strides and jumped on him, wrapping my legs around his middle and my arms around his neck, kissing him hard.

He kissed me back. The sacks he was holding crackled as he hurried to wrap his arms around me.

When I pulled away, he smiled. "What was that for?"

"I don't know. I just needed to."

"You should follow your gut more often," he said, kissing me again.

He asked me to drive, and five hours after I left work, I pulled into Gina's driveway. There were two police cars and another car, dark blue with the Oklahoma Department of Human Services logo on the driver and passenger doors.

"Oh my God," I said. I turned to Weston. "I don't know what this is about, but you have to go."

He shook his head. "No way. We're getting through everything together now, remember?"

Hot tears burned my eyes. "I appreciate that. I really do, but this is humiliating. I don't want you to hear whatever they have to say."

"What are they going to say?"

"I don't know, but I don't want you to hear it."

Weston hesitated, and then grabbed my hand gently. "Does she hit you?" I shook my head, and Weston sighed with relief. "When are you going to learn that I don't judge you, Erin? I love everything about you. I always have." When I didn't respond, he squeezed my hand. "Let me come with you. Please?"

I nodded and turned off the engine. We both walked to my house, hand in hand. When we walked in, Gina was sitting on the couch, her expression blank. Two police officers were standing to the side, and a woman from DHS was sitting next to her. She smiled at me.

"Hi, Erin. My name is Kay Rains. I'm from the Department of Human Services. We've come because of certain circumstances regarding the death of Erin Alderman."

"Okay…" I said, completely confused. Did they think her death had something to do with me?

She smiled, noticing my nervousness. "It's okay, Erin. You're not in any trouble."

"What's with the cops, then?" Weston asked. His hand was still firmly holding mine.

Kay nodded. "We didn't mean to frighten you. It's just procedure. We need you to come to the hospital with us. There is some confusion."

I frowned. "With the Erins? What does that have to do with me?"

Kay stood. "An autopsy was requested for Erin Alderman. The results were returned last night, and the parents have questions. If we could just get a blood sample from you, we can get all of this cleared up."

"A blood sample? You still haven't said what this has to do with Erin," Weston said.

Kay sighed. "The results have shown that Erin Alderman is not the biological child of Sam and Julianne Alderman. Erin Masterson's results are normal. You're the only female baby that was born at Blackwell Hospital on September fourth. In fact, you're the only baby that was born, besides the girls that passed away, within three days of your birthdays."

"Are you saying that you think Erin Alderman is Gina Easter's daughter, and Erin is… Sam and Julianne's?" Weston said. We both gasped when he finished his last word.

Kay touched Gina's knee, even though she wasn't visibly upset. "Unfortunately, that is what we suspect."

Weston and I looked at each other, both of our mouths hanging open.

"I'll…uh…I'll drive you."

I nodded.

"We'll return her shortly, Ms. Easter."

Gina nodded, and we all left her alone in the living room.

My shoes crunched against the gravel as we walked to Weston's truck. He opened the door and picked me up, sitting me in the passenger seat without effort. He looked straight into my eyes.

"Is this for real?" he asked.

I shook my head, unable to speak.

Weston got behind the wheel, and followed the DHS car and the two police cruisers to the hospital. We were escorted to the lab, and then sat in the waiting room. Weston held my hand. I stared at the white tile floor, unable to speak, or even think. My brain felt stuck, as if it wouldn't allow me to even explore the possibility of what all this meant.

"Erin Easter," the tech said. I stood up, and Weston stood up with me.

"Just her, please," Kay said.

I nodded to Weston and he sat.

The tech led me through the door into a small room with cabinets and a counter top. He gathered a long rubber strap and clear tubes on a silver tray next to me. I looked away, letting him stab me with the needle, feeling him move just slightly as he switched out the tubes. He extracted the needle, placed a cotton swab on the puncture site, and taped it down with a hot pink, sticky material that looked like a piece of ace bandage.

I stepped out to find Weston standing in the waiting room, between Kay and the police officers. "What now?" I asked.

Kay offered a sweet, reassuring grin and handed me her card. "And now we wait. If you need anything at all, call my cell phone. It's listed on the card. I'll come by with the results the moment we have them. We put a rush on the order, but they're sending them off, so it will likely be Wednesday."

"Oh. I don't have a…"

Weston took the card, looked at the number, and then tapped his phone. "I've got it," he said. He tapped his phone again and waited. Kay's phone rang, and she dug it from her purse and looked down. "That's me," Weston said. "You can reach her at this number."

Kay and the officers walked in front of us as we headed down the hall toward the parking lot. They backed out before we buckled our seat belts.

"Do you…do you think it's possible? That Gina's not my…" Just saying the words took my breath away, and my mind shut down again. It wouldn't let me process the possibility.

Weston intertwined his fingers with mine. I don't know how my luck changed so dramatically, but this had to be an apology straight from God. If Weston hadn't been sitting next to me, holding my hand with that look of reassurance, I might have broken down.

I think you're coming home with me, that's what I think. We're going to put on sweats, eat junk food, and watch as many movies on demand as we can fit into one night.

My lips curled up. That sounded a lot like what we'd been doing all Spring Break, and that was exactly what I needed. My smile faded. "Should I go home? Talk to Gina?"

"Do you want to?"

I shook my head. "I don't think anything good will come out of it. So I guess not."

Weston turned south and drove down Thirteenth Street, in the direction of his house. I had spent most of my time the last nine days either at the Dairy Queen or Weston's. Gina hadn't even asked any questions or spoken to me at all. Not that I was complaining. Spring Break had been the best week of my life, and the thought had crossed my mind more than once that I wouldn't mind if things stayed that way forever.

Once the truck was in the garage, Weston turned off the engine and pushed the garage door button. We walked down the hallway to find Peter and Veronica sitting at the table. Peter was in a dark gray suit with a black tie, and Veronica was in a beautiful black dress with a black belt.

She stood and crossed the tile floor, her heels clicking with each step. She hugged her son for several moments, then let him go, dabbing her nose with a tissue. "Where have you been?" She wasn't angry, but she was clearly emotionally drained. Her eyes scanned me, more curious than before.

"We've been driving around mostly, but we just got back from the…" Weston glanced back at me, waiting for permission to continue.

"The hospital," I said. "I was asked to give a blood sample."

Weston took my hand. "They requested an autopsy for Alder. She isn't Sam and Julianne's biological daughter."

His parents weren't surprised.

"We heard," Veronica said.

"Is it true?" Peter asked. "Sam and Jillian just left here."

"Left *here*?" I asked.

Veronica sniffed. "They've suffered the unimaginable as parents, and now it's happening again. I'm not sure if I'm just exhausted, or...she has Jillian's eyes, Peter. Don't you think?"

Peter shook his head. "Veronica. Don't get the girl's hopes up."

I frowned. "Get my hopes up? As if this is a prize that I'm waiting to win? Do you really think this would be a good thing?"

Veronica and Peter looked at each other, then Weston, then at me. "Sam and Julianne are wonderful people, Erin. If it's true, you'll have a whole new, amazing family to look forward to," Peter said.

"If it's true, that means I've missed out on eighteen years with them. I'm not sure I want it to be true. For me or for them."

Veronica crossed her arms across her stomach, and Peter put his arm around her. It was odd, because they were mirroring Weston and me.

Peter nodded. "You're right, Erin. It's a horrible situation for all of you. We're so sorry."

I shook my head. "No, I'm sorry. It's just been a very long day."

"Of course it has, honey," she said, leaving her husband's arms and reaching out for me. She clutched me to her and held me tight.

I glanced over at Weston, who was watching his mother with a look in his eyes that appeared to be a combination of appreciation and relief.

Veronica let me go with a smile on her face.

"We're going downstairs," Weston said.

He took my hand in his and led me to the basement. We sat on the couch, and Weston held up the remote, pushing the power button. The screen lit up, and he switched on the first movie listed. We settled in, neither of us feeling like we needed to have a lengthy conversation. In the last month, for both of us, life had gone from hopeless to happy, in the strangest, most unfortunate way.

10.

THE ROOM WAS QUIET WHEN I sat in my seat at the black table in first period. Everyone was staring at the floor, but when I walked in, they all glared at me. Then the whispering started. This was all very new, and I didn't know what to expect, which was more frightening than life before the Erins were dead.

For the first time in eighteen and a half years, I was the only Erin. There was no need for nicknames, and I didn't have to pretend not to notice Weston when he walked into the room. But that didn't change the way people felt about me. Brady's eyes twitched, the hateful words he wanted to say on the tip of his tongue.

The bell rang, but Mrs. Merit didn't speak. Instead, a crackling came over the speakers, and Principal Bringham came over the PA system.

"Good morning, students. As you all know, we lost two very bright students over Spring

Break, Erin Alderman and Erin Masterson. We're going to observe two minutes of silence today, for you to pray for their friends and family if you would like, or, if not, a moment of silent reflection."

The PA fell silent, and we all sat, staring at the floor. I was not the only person the Erins had relentlessly picked on, and certainly not the only one feeling a sense of relief more than a sense of loss. But, wherever they were, I hoped they were free of whatever plagued them to make others miserable, so they could feel better about themselves.

"Thank you," Principal Bringham said, and then the PA system shut off.

"I was asked to instruct all of you that if you need to speak to anyone about what happened to Sonny and Alder there are counselors here all week to help you understand and process your feelings. Now, please open your text books to page one eighty-eight."

Throughout the day, I noticed that the student body was mostly quiet. Occasionally one of the cheerleaders could be heard making a scene near their lockers. After Chrissy wailed after second period, they all seemed to try to outdo one another's outbursts of hysteria.

Brady was sandwiched between two empty chairs in Health class, and although I caught him glaring at Weston and me several times, he didn't say anything.

In Art class, Mrs. Cup called Weston to her desk, and they had a long, quiet conversation. It seemed like it ended well, but it ran so close to the end of the hour, that she was barely able to brief us on our last project: adding to the Blackwell mural downtown. The former Art teacher, Mrs. Boyer began the tradition, and Mrs. Cup continued it after Mrs. Boyer retired. We added our own tiny pieces, but mostly we filled in bits of brick that had broken off, or painted what had worn away over the last year.

"Be prepared," Mrs. Cup said. "We'll be going to the mural site tomorrow. Be sure to bring your things with you, so you don't have to come back to the building. You can leave straight from the mural at 3:30."

Weston sat in his stool at my desk.

"Is she still going to fail you?" I whispered.

He shook his head and tried not to smile.

Two girls stood in Mrs. Cup's open doorway. "Mrs. Cup, Mr. Bringham needs to see Erin Easter."

"All right," Mrs. Cup said, gesturing for me to gather my things.

"He said he needed for her to come right away," one of the girls added.

I gathered my things, and Weston touched my arm. "Do you want me to come with you?"

"I'll be okay."

He frowned. "I want to come with you."

I grinned. "You worry too much. You don't have to protect me, Weston."

"Says who?" he said, only half joking. "I'll wait for you in the front."

I shook my head. "You'll be late for practice. Go ahead."

He watched me as I stuffed a few things in my backpack. I followed the girls down the hall. We passed the set of lockers that stood alone in the middle of the commons area and then turned left toward the office. Just a few weeks before, I'd gone down this way, soaking wet. Now life seemed completely different, and it felt like it was about to change more.

I walked into the office, where Kay Rains stood, along with a police officer, Principal Bringham, and the counselor, Mrs. Rodgers. A few students and teachers idled about or sat in a row of chairs beside the door, waiting for something. Maybe for me, and whatever was about to happen.

"Why don't we step into my office?" Principal Bringham said. "I think that would be best."

Our small group followed him, and Kay asked me to sit with her in one of the two chairs in front of the principal's desk. Mr. Bringham sat down and clasped his hands in front of him.

"Erin, I understand you've taken a blood test. Do you understand why?"

I nodded.

"I don't want you to be nervous. I know there are a lot of people in here, but it's just a formality. Ms. Rains has the test results, and she's come here to explain them to you."

"With a police officer?" I asked.

Kay chuckled. "I know. It's awful. But we felt it was best since we're on school grounds and the potential for emotions to run high…it seems like a bit much to me as well. But because you're eighteen, and Ms. Easter requested we inform you at school should the results come back a certain way, we've come here."

"I don't mean to be rude, but can we get to the point? I'm going to be late for work."

Kay blinked. "Of course, I'm sorry." She shifted in her seat. "Erin, according to the test results on all three of you girls, we've come to the conclusion that there was a mistake at the hospital the day you were born. It appears that the late Miss Alderman was given to the Aldermans, and you were given to Ms. Easter…by mistake."

Mrs. Rodgers side stepped, making eye contact with me. "What she's trying to say, Erin, is that you are Sam and Julianne Alderman's biological daughter. Now, you're eighteen, so I'm not sure what this means to you, but the Aldermans have been informed, and they would very much like to speak with you as soon as you're ready."

"They know?"

Mrs. Rodgers nodded and smiled. "And they're eager to talk to you about it, if that's all right. They know this is a huge shock for you, and they want to give you as much space as you need to think this over."

"Where's Gina?" I asked.

Kay looked to Mrs. Rodgers, then to me. "She opted out of the meeting. She has been made aware, as well."

I thought for a moment, while everyone in the room waited for my reaction. I looked at

Mr. Bringham from under my brow. "Am I free to go?"

"Of course. This must be very upsetting for you. Mrs. Rodgers and I are available to talk when you're ready."

Mrs. Rodgers knelt next to my chair. "If you have any questions, legal or otherwise, I would be happy to help you, Erin. Please don't hesitate."

I stood up and took my backpack with me. "Thank you. I appreciate It, but I have to go to work now."

The police officer moved to the side and opened the door, and I walked out, trying to ignore the dozen or so pairs of eyes staring at me. I pushed through the side door of the building, to find Weston's truck sitting under the overhang in the half-circle drive in front of the school.

I walked past him, but he jumped out and jogged after me. "What did they say?" When I didn't respond or stop, Weston stood in front of me.

I blinked.

"Erin. What did they say to you?"

"That Gina Easter isn't my mother, and Julianne Alderman is."

Weston stood up straight and looked over my head, lost in thought. "Whoa." He looked back down at me. "Are you okay?"

"I need to walk."

"Sure you don't want me to drive you? Let me drive you."

I took a deep breath. "I haven't walked in a while, and right now I just really, really need to walk."

Weston nodded, and I walked around him, concentrating on putting one foot in front of the other until my feet hit the familiar asphalt in front of the Dairy Queen. I yanked open the door and slipped on my apron, tying it quickly as I made my way to the front.

Frankie was taking a bite from her own concoction, leaning against the counter. "I thought maybe you weren't coming in today."

"Sorry. I had a meeting."

"With Weston?"

"No," I said, frowning.

"He was about ten feet behind you when you came into view, driving about one mile per hour, and then he turned into the ball fields and ran in to practice. Did you dump him?"

"We're not…together…really."

"So you dumped him?"

"No."

"What kind of meeting?"

"With the principal and the counselor and some lady from DHS."

"Why?"

"I'm not really sure why she was there. They don't really know what to do."

"About what?"

"When, uh...Alder died...they did some tests, and they came back weird. So they did some tests on Sonny. Those were fine. So they asked me for a blood sample."

"I'm completely confused, but I think you're going to make sense any minute," Frankie said, shoveling the spoon of Whatever Blizzard into her mouth.

"So, they tell me today after school that Gina's not my mom."

"What?" Frankie said, standing up, her mouth still full of ice cream.

"And Gina's not even there. I mean...they said they told her, so she knows, but she wanted them to tell me at school. She didn't come to be there when they told me. So I don't know if I'm supposed to go get my stuff, or if I have a place to live, or..."

Frankie pulled me into her chest and wrapped her arms around me, and it was then that I realized I was sobbing.

"Baby girl," she said, rocking me ever so slightly from side to side. She pulled away and held my cheeks in her hands. "What are you doing here? You can't work like this."

"I don't have anywhere else to go!"

Frankie held me again, making soothing hush sounds like most mothers did. Except for mothers like Gina, who probably wasn't sure what she was more indifferent about—knowing she raised someone else's child, or that her biological child was dead.

The road was quiet, and not many people must have felt like ice cream, because we had only two customers by the time baseball practice let out, and Frankie waited on them both.

"He's going to drive straight over here. I bet he's been so distracted and dying to see you he could barely stand it," Frankie said.

I chewed my thumbnail, staring at the red Chevy parked across the street. "No way. Not after the way I treated him."

"Honey, if he can't understand that you had just gotten the shock of your life, then he doesn't deserve to see you."

The driver's side door of the Chevy opened and shut. The truck quickly backed out, paused for less than a second, and then surged across the street, not stopping until it was behind the Dairy Queen. I rushed to the back door, but Weston had already opened it.

I practically lunged for him, and he caught me, letting me squeeze the life out of him without complaint. He made the same soothing sounds Frankie was before and I cried again.

Frankie stood in the doorway, staring at me like I was dying. "Take that girl home, Weston."

"I don't...have a home," I said, bawling.

"I'm taking you home with me," Weston said. He placed me on my feet just long enough to lift me into his arms and carry me to the passenger side of his pickup. Frankie opened the door for him, and he set me in the seat and closed the door. Frankie's muffled voice buzzed and then paused as Weston spoke. After they hugged, he jogged around to the driver's side.

He held my hand firmly in his as we drove to his house, and again as we walked inside. He led me straight to the lower level and watched me as I sat on the couch.

"I'm going to run upstairs and grab some drinks and...what are you hungry for?"

"I'm not, really."

Weston sighed and nodded. "No, I imagine not." He pushed a button on the remote and started the last movie on the list, then hurried back up the stairs. I was glad he turned on the television before he went and didn't leave me alone with my thoughts.

Less than two minutes later, Weston was sitting next to me, placing the various boxes and packages he'd brought with him on the coffee table, including tissues. Then he twisted the cap on a bottle of Fanta, handing it to me.

"I figured you probably didn't need the caffeine."

My hand shook as I held the bottle to my lips and took a sip. Weston took the bottle from me and set it on the coffee table. When he settled back to the couch, I leaned against him, letting myself sink into his arms.

He touched his lips to my temple. "Tell me what to do, Erin. Tell me how to make you feel better," he whispered.

"This," I replied. "Just this."

11.

AT FIVE THIRTY, THE GARAGE
door hummed above us. We could hear the
door open and close, and other sounds that sig-
naled both of his parents were home. Before
long, the door at the top of the stairs opened,
and two sets of footsteps descended the stairs.

Weston didn't move, and neither did
I. Peter and Veronica each sat in one of two
recliners on each side of the coffee table. Peter
rested his elbows on his knees and clasped his
hands, reminding me of the principal right
before he told me the news.

"We heard," Peter said, his voice low and
calm.

Veronica leaned forward, pure sympathy in
her eyes. "Peter and I have been discussing this
since we heard, and when you're ready, we'd like
to offer you some legal advice. However, we've
also spoken to Sam and Julianne Alderman,

and they're hoping to speak with you at your earliest convenience."

"Like when?" I asked. I was lying against Weston and probably looked like an ill-mannered sloth, but I was emotionally and physically tapped.

"They live right around the corner from us," Peter said. "They're waiting at their home, now. They just want to make sure you're okay. It doesn't have to be tonight."

A door slammed upstairs and footsteps stomped all over the kitchen. "Veronica?" A female voice called. She sounded desperate.

Peter ran up the stairs. A calm disagreement ensued, and then several people came down to Weston's space, where no one was supposed to be bothering us. Weston and I both stood when we saw Sam and Julianne standing at the bottom of the stairs.

Peter was breathing hard. "Julianne, I don't think this is a good idea," he warned.

Julianne's eyes were bright red. She began to walk over to me, but her husband stopped her.

"Julianne!"

Julianne held her hands in front of her chest. "I'm so sorry. I know you've had an upsetting day. I just…I've had one, too. An upsetting week, actually, and I…" a tear escaped her eye and fell down her cheek. "I heard that you didn't have a lot of support at the school when you were told the news, and I…just needed to make sure that you're okay. That's all I wanted to do."

I took a few steps until I was a couple of feet away from them: my parents. They were gawking at me like a precious gem. Sam held on to Julianne's shoulders, and she nearly leaned forward.

She held out her hands, and then made them into fists, clearly fighting with what she wanted and what she should do. Her voice broke when she spoke. "Would it be okay if I…I would just like to hug you, if that's okay. I don't want to upset you."

Everyone watched me for my response.

Almost too subtly for anyone to see, I nodded once, and Julianne reached for me, pulling me against her chest. Her body shook as she sobbed.

"Julianne, honey," Sam begged. "Please don't scare her."

I looked up at him from her shoulder. "It's okay. She can cry."

Sam's lips trembled, and he reached out, hesitant and nervous, and touched my shoulder. Tears streamed down his cheeks as well, and the corners of his mouth curled up as he watched his wife hold me while she cried.

An hour later, we were all upstairs, sitting at the table around a half-eaten cheese and cracker tray, an empty bottle of wine, and a two-liter bottle of Fanta Orange, minus two glasses poured. Peter and Veronica talked about their ski vacation, and how Peter's skiing skills weren't quite as advanced as he thought.

It felt good to laugh, to listen to Sam and Julianne talk, and to get to know them better. I couldn't stop staring at them. Veronica was right; I did have Julianne's eyes. And for the first time, I associated myself with beauty, because I always thought that Julianne Alderman was beautiful, inside and out. The bottom half of my face was from Sam. I had the same thin top lip with the M-shape in the center, and the full bottom lip. I also had his chin. I wondered if they thought the same things about me, or if anyone had ever thought these things about me.

Julianne reached across the table and held my hands. "You must think I'm a horrible mother, for not knowing. I'm a PA for goodness sake. But I told them, when they didn't bring you back to me after your bath, that they had brought back the wrong baby. I knew, but they said I was just tired. Then they said it was the hormones. And through the years, other mothers said they had the same fears because of the stories you hear."

"Julianne, I think it's time we let Erin rest. She has school tomorrow."

Julianne held her hand to her chest, fumbling with the buttons on her silk blouse; then she began to tremble. "I…I don't know if she… do you want to…?"

"Why doesn't she stay here for the night?" Veronica said. "After she calls Ms. Easter and lets her know where she is?"

"We don't have a phone," I said. "And she doesn't really…I don't think she's expecting me."

That seemed to upset Julianne.

"We have some of Whitney's clothes still here. You're welcome to them," Veronica said.

"Do you want to stay here?" Julianne asked.

"I would appreciate that," I said, feeling emotional again.

Sam stood and encouraged Julianne to stand with him. She clearly didn't want to leave, but he encouraged her until she finally yielded, but not without giving me another hug.

When the door closed, Weston, Veronica, Peter, and I stood in the front room, looking at each other.

"Erin, you can stay in Whitney's old room. This is a bit...unorthodox, but I think it's in your best interest until Sam and Julianne and you decide where to go from here. From a legal standpoint, this is all a little fuzzy since you're no longer a minor. Don't worry. You're Sam and Julianne's daughter. Whatever you decide, they're going to make sure you're well taken care of. Weston, show her to her room. Let her rest. She's had a long day."

Weston nodded and led me up the stairs by the hand. Whitney's room was on the opposite end of the hall from Weston's. She had her own enormous bathroom, with a tub and shower and a linen cabinet that spanned from floor to ceiling, full of big, fluffy towels. Weston checked to make sure there was soap and shampoo.

"We can pick up anything else you need from Gina's tomorrow, if you want."

I dipped my head in agreement.

He led me back into the bedroom, and pulled back the comforter. "Clean sheets." He opened the closet. "Clothes and lots of 'em." He pulled open a dresser drawer. "Night gowns and pajama sets. Some of them silk, because Whitney's a huge diva. Just leave your laundry in that hamper and Lila will launder them in the morning when she gets here. I'm pretty sure Whitney still has makeup and ponytail holders and stuff in the drawers by the sink."

"She does," Veronica said, breezing through the door. She handed me a new toothbrush, a full tube of toothpaste, and a brand new stick of deodorant. "Peter is always saying I overstock. You have won a twenty-year-long argument for me tonight, little miss."

"I wish I could think of a way to say thank you. I'm sorry I…"

"Nonsense," Veronica said, holding the knob while she hovered in the doorway. "We're going to get this all worked out. You try to rest. See you in the morning. Wes?"

Weston leaned over and gave me a peck, and then followed his mother out. I walked into the spacious, sparkling white bathroom and undressed in front of the mirror. I took a long, hot shower, trying every brand name shampoo, conditioning treatment, and foaming face wash I could get my hands on. By the time I stepped out, I smelled like a salon, and my skin shone like the marble tile. I felt like Julia Roberts's character in *Pretty Woman*.

I wrapped myself in one of the fluffy towels and combed out my hair, noticing how close it was to Julianne's color. I found a nightgown and slipped it over my head, then climbed into the queen-sized bed. The springs didn't squeak when I laid on it. I wasn't even sure Whitney's bed had springs. It felt like one big foam-filled cushion. I rested my head on the pillow, stretching my legs as far as they would go. They didn't even come close to the end of the bed. My body sank down into the mattress, and the plush comforter cradled me in softness.

I turned on my side and leaned over, switching off the lamp. Before I could settle back under the blankets, the door opened, and Weston crept inside.

"Are you sleeping?" he whispered.

"No."

He knelt beside the bed. "Are you comfortable?"

"More than I've ever been."

"Do you need anything else before I hit the sack?"

I shook my head.

"I don't know if I can sleep knowing you're right down the hall."

I smiled. "Try."

He chuckled and leaned down, giving me a better kiss than he could when his mother was still around. He walked to the door and turned around. "You're going to be okay. This is just one more thing we'll get through together."

"I know." It should have been scarier, being eighteen and finding out that the woman who raised me wasn't my mother. But at the moment, I felt like I had a small army in my corner.

* * *

The next morning when I walked into school, it was like I was walking into a different dimension. Everyone stared at me like before, but now it was out of curiosity. In first period, Brady glanced over at me a few times, but the disgust was gone from his eyes. Even the teachers looked at me differently. It was like I left the day before as one person, and came back as someone else.

No one, not even Brady, called me Easter. If they addressed me, they called me Erin. For the first time in nine years, no one said a single negative word to me or even shot me a dirty look. I still expected it, waiting for someone, anyone to taunt me, but it never happened; not once all day. The rest of the week went that way, too, and by Friday, the tension I felt every time I walked into a classroom was gone, and I no longer waited for someone to throw insults or wads of paper at me. My thoughts were consumed by Weston, and Sam and Julianne. They had come over every night that week for dinner, and were coming over for dinner again after I left work Saturday evening. I couldn't pinpoint why, but this time it felt important.

On Saturday, Weston gave me a ride to work, and then drove across the street to warm up at the ball fields. He had a home game in a few hours that I wasn't happy about missing, but thankfully the scoreboard was visible over the wall. I tied the apron strings behind my back, and walked to the front, greeting Frankie with a smile.

"I thought you had a closet full of designer clothes to choose from," Frankie said.

"I don't want to wear that stuff to work. I don't want to ruin it." Lila had been washing and drying one of my two pairs of jeans every evening before she left for the day so I could pack them in my book bag and change into them for work. A lot of Whitney's clothes were very feminine and very expensive. Her shoes were a half size too big, but I didn't complain. This was the first time I'd worn brand name anything, much less designer clothes, but at work, I wore my worn, secondhand jeans and shirts.

We were slow for a Saturday, and Frankie and I passed the time discussing her kids, but mostly we talked about my new living arrangements, and what my life was like now. She grinned at me a lot when I talked, and I know that she was happy for me, but there was a sadness in her eyes that I couldn't quite decipher.

"Are you happy?" she asked.

"I don't know. I think so. More than I have been before."

Her eyes softened. "Good. Did you get the rest of your things from Gina?"

"We stopped by Gina's on Tuesday. I wasn't sure about just walking in, so I knocked. She didn't answer, so I walked in."

"Did you get everything you needed?"

I nodded. I didn't mention to Frankie that Soul Asylum was playing loudly when I walked in, so I rushed through my room and the bathroom, grabbing anything I thought I'd need—my other pair of jeans, my toothbrush, a razor, the little bit of makeup that I owned, underwear, bras, and a sketch pad. I left behind everything else.

"What did Gina have to say to you? Anything?"

I looked over at the score board. The game had just started.

"Why don't you go over there and watch him? We're not busy."

"I need the hours."

Frankie winked. "No you don't. You're an Alderman now. They're going to take care of you, Erin. You can finally be a teenager for once."

I thought about that for a moment then smiled. Tossing my apron on the hook, I jogged across the street and walked into the stadium. I'd never been to a baseball game before.

Not many people were sitting in the bleachers besides a handful of students and the families of the players.

"Erin!" Weston was standing on the other side of the fence in his uniform and ball cap, his shaggy brown hair sticking out the bottom. He slipped his fingers through the wires of the fence, beaming.

I approached the fence. "Frankie let me off to watch your game."

"I'm going to have to step it up a notch then." He winked and jogged back to the dugout.

I spent my Saturday afternoon sitting on the bleachers, baking in the direct sun. It felt glorious. Weston made it to third base once, and the next time hit a home run. He played first base and got three players on the opposite team out. Once he even caught the ball right as it careened off the bat. The popping sound the ball made when it hit Weston's glove made my hand hurt, but he was all smiles, and they all ran in off the field.

When they got their things together and listened to the coach speak, Weston made his way up to the bleachers and gave me a peck, sitting next to me. It was the first time he'd kissed me in public, and I didn't miss the stares it garnered.

"What?"

"People are looking at us."

"Good."

"I'm going to go back and help Frankie. It'll get busy since the game is over."

Weston kissed me goodbye, and I walked across the street, bursting into the back door and tying on my apron with a big grin.

"Was it fun?" Frankie asked.

"It was amazing. They won! Weston was great."

Frankie nodded, and we worked without a break until close. We cleaned up quickly, because I would have to hurry and change and make it downstairs by the time Sam and Julianne brought over dinner at seven. I encouraged Weston to hurry as soon as I climbed up into the truck, and the second Weston pulled into the garage, I let go of his hand and darted up the stairs.

Thirty minutes later, I emerged, showered, shaven, and lotioned. Weston was sitting on the top stair, waiting for me. He stood when I walked out of Whitney's room. I smiled at him, but he didn't smile back.

"What's wrong?"

"Nothing," he said, finally forcing a smile. He leaned down and kissed my cheek, and then we walked downstairs together. Peter and Veronica were setting the table while Sam and Julianne were uncovering dishes and setting them in the center.

Julianne and Sam's eyes lit up when they saw me, and they both came over to give me a hug. We sat down to eat, and Weston and I chatted about our day. The adults asked us more specific questions about our assignments, and how we felt about certain school policies, which brought us to Weston's art project. It could have been small talk, but Sam and Julianne seemed genuinely interested and hung on to my every word.

"I would love to see it sometime," Julianne said.

"It's up in my room."

"The one you had framed?" Veronica said, a little surprised.

"Yeah," Weston said.

"But you'd been working on that for months, hadn't you?" his mother asked.

Weston looked over at me. "Yes."

Recognition lit Veronica's eyes, and she stifled a grin. She seemed to want to ask more, but didn't. We were all stuck in this strange situation. Weston's ex-girlfriend was Sam and Julianne's faux-daughter, who also happened to be recently deceased. It was hard to know what appropriate conversation was.

"This is…uncomfortable," I said.

Sam's eyebrows pulled in. "It's okay. This is such a rare circumstance, Erin. There's just no room for judgment. We're just happy that you're happy. That's all that matters to us."

By the time we finished the chocolate cheesecake, Julianne seemed nervous. During a lull in conversation, Sam took Julianne's hand, and her eyes glossed over.

"Erin," Sam said. "Julianne and I have been talking quite a bit this week, and although we know everything has happened very fast for all of us, we want to ask you if you would come and live in our home…until you go to college, or until you want to live on your own. We just feel we have a lot of catching up to do, and we'd love it if we could do it as a family."

My eyes danced between the both of them. They watched me with desperate hope in their eyes.

"You'll have your own room," Julianne said. "We've already gotten you a new bed, dresser, and linens. But we thought you might want to make it yours by choosing your own comforter and things, so I left a few catalogs on the bed," Julianne said. She held up her hand. "Not that I'm assuming you'll come to live with us. I just…didn't want you to think we'd offer you Alder's room. You'll have your own room, your own clothes, and your own things."

Sam leaned forward a bit and pushed up his glasses. "You don't have to make a decision tonight. We just want you to know the offer is there. And we're not doing anything at all this weekend, just in case you want to, you know, move in. But again, no pressure."

"It's okay. I think it'd be good," I said.

"You do?" Julianne said, in shock.

I nodded.

Julianne clapped excitedly and they both stood, rushing around the table to hug me. Veronica and Peter congratulated us, and happy embraces were given all around, except for Weston.

I sat down, next to him. "Everything okay?" I asked.

"I'm just going to miss seeing you every day," he said.

"Weston, honey, she's right down the street!" Veronica said, laughing.

"I know," he said, still unhappy.

"I promise we'll be considerate of your time with her," Julianne assured him.

That seemed to cheer Weston up a bit, and he took my hand in his.

Sam and Julianne returned to their seats.

"When?" I asked. "I don't really have a lot to bring over."

"Tomorrow?" Julianne asked.

"Tomorrow?" I echoed.

"Or not," Sam sat, patting Julianne's knee. "When you're ready."

"I guess tomorrow is as good a time as any. If you're sure…"

Julianne didn't hesitate. "We're sure."

"Okay, then," I said with a small smile.

"Perfect!" Julianne said. "We'll take care of everything. If there is something you need that we don't have, you just let us know."

"So…to tomorrow?" Sam said, holding up his nearly empty wineglass. The other adults in the room held up their glasses, and Weston and I held up our glasses of Cherry Coke.

"To tomorrow," we all said in unison.

12.

SAM AND JULIANNE RETURNED home, anxious to finish up a few things before I moved in the next day. Peter and Veronica retreated to their bedroom, and Weston asked me to take a drive. We held hands while he drove out to his favorite spot, the overpass, and we lay in the bed of the truck, looking up at the stars.

"I'm a little nervous. I just got you, and I've had you all to myself until now," he said, leaning over to kiss my hair.

I leaned into his kiss, my head resting on his arm. "I'm just around the corner, and I'll still need a ride to school every morning. I don't think things will be that different."

"I don't know. You have eighteen years of making up to do, and I would be a complete ass if I begrudged you getting to know your parents. I feel like I should step aside, but I don't want to."

"I don't want you to step aside," I said, thinking over his last words. "My parents. Wow. It's just...*crazy*. I keep thinking I'm going to wake up, or someone's going to tell me this was a cruel prank."

"A cruel prank? You've just hit the lottery. Not only are your bullies gone, but you have two of the best people in town as your parents."

"It feels wrong to celebrate it."

"You didn't steal them, Erin. They're yours. Kind of like me."

I looked over at him, and I could see his amazing smile in the dim light of the moon. "It's just too much good luck all at once for someone who hasn't had any. I feel like it's all going to be ripped away from me at any moment."

"I'm not going anywhere," he said. "I promise."

I turned onto my side, leaning over him, and touched my lips to his. It was a chilly night, but something deep inside of me felt warm, and the warmth spread throughout my body. Weston felt it, too, because his fingers pressed into my skin, and he made that little sound that I loved. I pulled away, and bit my lip, a little nervous about what I was about to do.

I sat up, and slipped my shirt over my head. Weston didn't move until I reached back to unsnap my bra, and then he sat up, grabbing my arms. He kissed me once, whispering against my lips.

"What are you doing?" His eyes were closed, but the tension of restraint was evident in every muscle of his body.

"What does it look like I'm doing?"

"Not here."

"What?"

"You don't want your first time to be in the back of my truck."

"Why not? My favorite memories are here."

He thought about it for a moment. When I kissed him, he kissed me back, hard. His fingers touched the top of my shoulders, and he pulled down the white straps of my bra. The second it was lying next to us, he ripped his shirt over his head and pulled me against him. His warm chest against my bare breasts created a tingling between my thighs, and it was my turn to make that low humming sound.

Weston turned me onto my back, undid my jeans, and pulled them down, past my ankles, and set them in the pile with the rest of our clothes. It didn't take long for both of us to be naked, and then Weston was above me, his mouth on mine, his bare skin against mine.

I squeezed his hips between my thighs while he slipped on a condom, but when he was finished and perfectly positioned to take my virginity, he paused.

"Are you sure?" he asked. "I mean completely sure. You can say wait right now, and I'd be okay with it. I'll wait."

I reached down to his bare backside, and with my fingers, pushed him into me. He buried his face in my neck as he worked his way in, gentle and slow. I was glad he wasn't kissing me, because I was unable to focus on anything but the uncomfortable burning. After a few minutes, though, we seemed to fit together perfectly, and I relaxed. Weston's mouth returned to mine, and we touched and tasted each other until we were spent.

Just before sunrise, Weston reached for his jeans pocket. He pulled out his inhaler and took a puff. He stared at me, exhausted and happy. We settled on our backs, looking up at the stars. Weston kissed my forehead and reached over to his jacket, covering me. He reached for his jeans pocket, pulling out a long, black box.

"I got you something," he said.

"For what?"

"Your birthday."

"My birthday was in September," I said.

He chuckled. "It's a belated birthday gift. I wanted to wait until graduation, but I couldn't. Now feels like the perfect moment."

The box creaked when I peeled it apart, and my hands trembled with excitement. It had been a long time since anyone had given me anything. The lid flipped open, revealing a silver heart. It was nearly identical to the one in the charcoal drawing, complete with *Happenstance* etched across it. I gasped.

"Do you like it?" he asked.

"*Like* it? It's the same necklace, isn't it?"

He beamed. "You remembered."

"Of course I remembered, how did you find this?"

We both sat up. Weston pulled the necklace from the box and fastened the clasp behind my neck. "I have connections. I'm a good person to know, you know."

"I know," I said, wrapping my arms around him.

He kissed me once. "I didn't know that when I saw it on you, it would be the only thing you were wearing. This is a definite bonus."

I giggled.

He looked at the heart, then back up at me. "It's perfect. Like the girl in the window."

"She's not perfect," I said, shaking my head.

"She's perfect for me." He touched his lips to mine, and just when that warm, tingling feeling began to spread throughout my body, he pulled away.

"We'd better get dressed and get you back to the house so we can get a few hours of sleep. We've got to get you moved today."

"I'm moving in with the Aldermans," I said, thinking out loud.

"You *are* an Alderman."

I shook my head, in complete disbelief. "This is going to mess with my head if I think about it too hard."

Weston helped me from the tailgate, and again to the passenger side of his truck. It was beginning to feel like *my* side, and I liked that. He held my hand as he drove me back to his house, and I felt at ease knowing that even though I was leaving that day, I would be only a few houses away.

Weston noticed that I was lost in thought and squeezed my hand. "Try not to overthink it. It is what it is."

I touched the necklace that hung perfectly against the little indention between my collar bones, and wondered what it would be like to live as Erin Alderman.

"It's happenstance," I whispered.

1.

His words hung there, in the darkness between our voices. I sometimes found comfort in that space, but in three months, I'd only found unrest. That space became more like a convenient place to hide. Not for me, for him. My fingers ached, so I allowed them to relax, not realizing how hard I'd been gripping my cell phone.

My roommate, Raegan, was sitting next to my open suitcase on the bed, her legs crisscrossed. Whatever look was on my face prompted her to take my hand. *T.J.?* she mouthed.

I nodded.

"Will you please say something?" T.J. asked.

"What do you want me to say? I'm packed. I took vacation time. Hank has already given Jorie my shifts."

"I feel like a huge asshole. I wish I didn't have to go, but I warned you. When I have an ongoing project, I can be called out at any time. If you need help with rent or anything…"

"I don't want your money," I said, rubbing my eyes.

"I thought this would be a good weekend. I swear to God I did."

"I thought I'd be getting on a plane tomorrow morning, and instead you're calling me to say I can't come. Again."

"I know this seems like a dick move. I swear to you I told them I had important plans. But when things come up, Cami…I have to do my job."

I wiped a tear from my cheek, but I refused to let him hear me cry. I kept the trembling from my voice. "Are you coming home for Thanksgiving, then?"

He sighed. "I want to. But I don't know if I can. It depends on if this is wrapped up. I do miss you. A lot. I don't like this, either."

"Will your schedule ever get better?" I asked. It took him longer than it should to answer.

"What if I said probably not?"

I lifted my eyebrows. I expected that answer but didn't expect him to be so...truthful.

"I'm sorry," he said. I imagined him cringing. "I just pulled into the airport. I have to go."

"Yeah, okay. Talk to you later." I forced my voice to stay level. I didn't want to sound upset. I didn't want him to think I was weak or emotional. He was strong, and self-reliant, and did what had to be done without complaint. I tried to be that for him. Whining about something out of his control wouldn't help anything.

He sighed again. "I know you don't believe me, but I do love you."

"I believe you," I said, and I meant it.

I pressed the red button on the screen and let my phone fall to the bed.

Raegan was already in damage control mode. "He was called into work?"

I nodded.

"Okay, well, maybe you guys will just have to be more spontaneous. Maybe you can just show up, and if he's called out while you're there, you wait on him. When he gets back, you pick up where you left off."

"Maybe."

She squeezed my hand. "Or maybe he's a tool who should stop choosing his job over you?"

I shook my head. "He's worked really hard for this position."

"You don't even know what position it is."

"I told you. He's utilizing his degree. He specializes in statistical analysis and data reconfiguration, whatever that means."

She shot me a dubious look. "Yeah, you also told me to keep it all a secret. Which makes me think he's not being completely honest with you."

I stood up and dumped out my suitcase, letting all the contents spill onto my comforter. Usually I only made my bed when I was packing, so I could now see the comforter's light blue fabric with a few navy blue octopus tentacles reaching across it. T.J. hated it, but it made me feel like I was being hugged while I slept. My room was made up of strange, random things, but then, so was I.

Raegan rummaged through the pile of clothes, and held up a black top with the shoulders and front strategically ripped. "We both have the night off. We should go out. Get drinks served to us for once."

I grabbed the shirt from her hands and inspected it while I mulled over Raegan's suggestion. "You're right. We should. Are we taking your car, or the Smurf?"

Raegan shrugged. "I'm almost on empty and we don't get paid until tomorrow."

"Looks like it's the Smurf, then."

After a crash session in the bathroom, Raegan and I jumped up into my light blue, modified CJ Jeep. It wasn't in the best of shape, but at one time, someone had enough vision and love to mold it into a Jeep/truck hybrid. The spoiled college dropout who owned the Smurf between that owner and me didn't love it as much. The seat cushions were exposed in some places where the black leather seats were torn, the carpet had cigarette holes and stains, and the hard top needed to be replaced, but that neglect meant that I could pay for it in full, and a payment-free vehicle was the best kind to own.

I buckled my seat belt, and stabbed the key into the ignition.

"Should I pray?" Raegan asked.

I turned the key, and the Smurf made a sickly whirring noise. The engine sputtered, and then purred, and we both clapped. My parents raised four children on a factory worker's salary. They didn't buy a vehicle for any of my brothers, despite their appeals, so I knew it was the right choice not to even bother asking. I got a job at the local ice cream shop when I was fifteen, and saved $557.11. The Smurf wasn't the vehicle I dreamed about when I was little, but 550 bucks bought me independence, and that was priceless.

Twenty minutes later, Raegan and I were on the opposite side of town, strutting across the gravel lot of the Red Door, slowly and in unison, as if we were being filmed while walking to a badass soundtrack.

Kody was standing at the entrance, his huge arms probably the same size as my head. He eyed us as we approached. "IDs."

"Fuck off!" Raegan snarled. "We work here. You know how old we are."

He shrugged. "Still have to see IDs."

I frowned at Raegan, and she rolled her eyes, digging into her back pocket. "If you don't know how old I am at this point, we have issues."

"C'mon, Raegan. Quit busting my balls and let me see the damn thing."

"The last time I let you see something you didn't call me for three days."

He cringed. "You're never going to get over that, are you?"

She tossed her ID at Kody and he slapped it against his chest. He glanced at it, and then handed it back, looking at me expectantly. I handed him my driver's license.

"Thought you were leaving town?" he asked, glancing down before returning the thin plastic card to me.

"Long story," I said, stuffing my license into my back pocket. My jeans were so tight I was amazed I could fit anything besides my ass back there.

Kody opened the oversize red door, and Raegan smiled sweetly. "Thanks, baby."

"Love you. Be good."

"I'm always good," she said, winking.

"See you when I get off work?"

"Yep." She pulled me through the door.

"You are the weirdest couple," I said over the bass. It was buzzing in my chest, and I was fairly certain every beat made my bones shake.

"Yep," Raegan said again.

The dance floor was already packed with sweaty, drunk college kids. The fall semester was in full swing. Raegan walked over to the bar and stood at the end. Jorie winked at her.

"Want me to clear you out some seats?" she asked.

Raegan shook her head. "You're just offering because you want my tips from last night!"

Jorie laughed. Her long, platinum blond hair fell in loose waves past her shoulders, with a few black peekaboo strands. She wore a black minidress and combat boots, and was pushing buttons on the cash register to ring someone up while she talked to us. We had all learned to multitask and move like every tip was a hundred-dollar bill. If you could bartend fast enough, you stood a chance of working the east bar, and the tips made there could pay a month's worth of bills in a weekend.

That was where I'd been tending bar for a year, placed just three months after I was hired at the Red Door. Raegan worked right beside me, and together we kept that machine greased like a stripper in a plastic pool full of baby oil. Jorie and the other bartender, Blia, worked the south bar at the entrance. It was basically a kiosk, and they loved it when Raegan or I were out of town.

"So? What are you drinking?" Jorie asked.

Raegan looked at me, and then back at Jorie. "Whiskey sours."

I made a face. "Minus the sour, please."

Once Jorie passed us our drinks, Raegan and I found an empty table and sat, shocked at our luck. Weekends were always packed, and an open table at ten thirty wasn't common.

I held a brand-new pack of cigarettes in my hand and hit the end of it against my palm to pack them, then tore off the plastic, flipping the top. Even though the Red was so smoky that just sitting there made me feel like I was smoking an entire pack of cigarettes, It was nice to sit at a table and relax. When I was working, I usually had time for one drag and the rest burned away, unsmoked.

Raegan watched me light it. "I want one."

"No, you don't."

"Yes, I do!"

"You haven't smoked in two months, Raegan. You'll blame me tomorrow for ruining your streak."

She gestured at the room. "I'm smoking! Right now!"

I narrowed my eyes at her. Raegan was exotically beautiful, with long, chestnut brown hair, bronze skin, and honey brown eyes. Her nose was perfectly small, not too round or too pointy, and her skin made her look like she came fresh off of a Neutrogena commercial. We met in elementary school, and I was instantly drawn to her brutal honesty. Raegan could be incredibly intimidating, even for Kody, who, at six foot four, was over a foot taller than she was. Her personality was charming to those she loved, and a repellant to those she didn't.

I was the opposite of exotic. My tousled brown bob and heavy bangs were easy to maintain, but not a lot of men found it sexy. Not a lot of men found me sexy in general. I was the girl next door, your brother's best friend. Growing up with three brothers and our cousin Colin, I could have been a tomboy if my subtle but still present curves hadn't ousted me from the boys' only clubhouse at fourteen.

"Don't be that girl," I said. "If you want one, go buy your own."

She crossed her arms, pouting. "That's why I quit. They're fucking expensive."

I stared at the burning paper and tobacco nestled between my fingers. "That is a fact my broke ass continues to make note of."

The song switched from something everyone wanted to dance to, to a song no one wanted to dance to, and dozens of people began making their way off the dance floor. Two girls walked up to our table and traded glances.

"That's our table," the blonde said.

Raegan barely acknowledged them.

"Excuse me, bitch she's talking to you," the brunette said, setting her beer on the table.

"Raegan," I warned.

Raegan looked at me with a blank face, and then up at the girl with the same expression. "It *was* your table. Now it's ours."

"We were here first," the blonde hissed.

"And now you're not," Raegan said. She picked up the unwelcome beer bottle and tossed it across the floor. It spilled out onto the dark, tightly stitched carpet. "Fetch."

The brunette watched her beer slide across the floor, and then took a step toward Raegan, but her friend grabbed both of her arms. Raegan offered an unimpressed laugh, and then turned her gaze toward the dance floor. The brunette finally followed her friend to the bar.

I took a drag from my cigarette. "I thought we were going to have a good time tonight."

"That was fun, right?"

I shook my head, stifling a smile. Raegan was a great friend, but I wouldn't cross her. Growing up with so many boys in the house,

I'd had enough fighting to last a lifetime. They didn't baby me. If I didn't fight back, they'd just fight dirtier until I did. And I always did.

Raegan didn't have an excuse. She was just a scrappy bitch. "Oh, look. Megan's here," she said, pointing to the blue-eyed, crow-headed beauty on the dance floor. I shook my head. She was out there with Travis Maddox, basically getting screwed in front of everyone on the dance floor.

"Oh, those Maddox boys," Raegan said.

"Yeah," I said, downing my whiskey. "This was a bad idea. I'm not feeling clubby tonight."

"Oh, stop." Raegan gulped her whiskey sour and then stood. "The whine bags are still eyeing this table. I'm going to get us another round. You know the beginning of the night starts off slow."

She took my glass and hers and left me for the bar.

I turned, seeing the girls staring at me, clearly hoping I would step away from the table. I wasn't about to stand up. Raegan would get the table back if they tried to take it, and that would only cause trouble.

When I turned around, a boy was sitting in Raegan's chair. At first I thought Travis had somehow made his way over, but when I realized my mistake, I smiled. Trenton Maddox was leaning toward me, his tattooed arms crossed, his elbows resting on the table across from me. He rubbed the five o'clock shadow that peppered his square jaw with his fingers, his shoulder muscles bulging through his T-shirt. He had as much stubble on his face as he did on the top of his head, except for the absence of hair from one small scar near his left temple.

"You look familiar."

I raised an eyebrow. "Really? You walk all the way over here and sit down, and that's the best you've got?"

He made a show of running his eyes over every part of me. "You don't have any tattoos, that I can see. I'm guessing we haven't met at the shop."

"The shop?"

"The ink shop I work at."

"You're tattooing now?"

He smiled, a deep dimple appearing in the center of his left cheek. "I knew we've met before."

"We haven't." I turned to watch the women on the dance floor, laughing and smiling and watching Travis and Megan vertically dry fucking. But the second the song was over, he left and walked straight over to the blonde who claimed ownership over my table. Even though she'd seen Travis running his hands all over Megan's sweaty skin two seconds earlier, she was grinning like an idiot, hoping she was next.

Trenton laughed once. "That's my baby brother."

"I wouldn't admit it," I said, shaking my head.

"Did we go to school together?" he asked.

"I don't remember."

"Do you remember if you went to Eakins at any time between kindergarten through twelfth grade?"

"I did."

Trenton's left dimple sunk in when he grinned. "Then we know each other."

"Not necessarily."

Trenton laughed again. "You want a drink?"

"I have one coming."

"You wanna dance?"

"Nope."

A group of girls passed by, and Trenton's eyes focused on one. "Is that Shannon from home ec? Damn," he said, turning a one-eighty in his seat.

"Indeed it is. You should go reminisce."

Trenton shook his head. "We reminisced in high school."

"I remember. Pretty sure she still hates you."

Trenton shook his head, smiled, and then, before taking another swig, said, "They always do."

"It's a small town. You shouldn't have burned all of your bridges."

He lowered his chin, his famous charm turning up a notch. "There's a few I haven't lit a fire under. Yet."

I rolled my eyes, and he chuckled.

Raegan returned, curving her long fingers around four standard rocks glasses and two shot glasses. "My whiskey sours, your whiskey straights, and a buttery nipple each."

"What is with all the sweet stuff tonight, Ray?" I said, wrinkling my nose.

Trenton picked up one of the shot glasses and touched it to his lips, tilting his head back. He slammed it on the table and winked. "Don't worry, babe. I'll take care of it." He stood up and walked away.

I didn't realize my mouth was hanging open until my eyes met Raegan's and it snapped shut.

"Did he just drink your shot? Did that really just happen?"

"Who does that?" I said, turning to see where he went. He'd already disappeared into the crowd.

"A Maddox boy."

I shot the double whiskey and took another drag of my cigarette. Everyone knew Trenton Maddox was bad news, but that never seemed to stop women from trying to tame him. Watching him since grade school, I promised myself that I would never be a notch on his headboard—if the rumors were true and he had notches, but I didn't plan to find out.

"You're going to let him get away with that?" Raegan asked.

I blew out the smoke from the side of my mouth, annoyed. I wasn't in the frame of mind to have fun, or deal with obnoxious flirting, or complain that Trenton Maddox had just drunk the shot glass of sugar that I didn't want. But before I could answer my friend, I had to choke back the whiskey I'd just drunk.

"Oh, no."

"What?" Raegan said, flipping around in her chair. She immediately righted herself in the chair, cringing.

All three of my brothers and our cousin Colin were walking toward our table.

Colin, the oldest and the only one with a legit ID, spoke first. "What the hell, Camille? I thought you were out of town tonight."

"My plans changed," I snapped.

Chase spoke second, as I expected he would. He was the oldest of my brothers, and liked to pretend he was older than me, too. "Why are you being so pissy? Are you on the rag or something?"

"Really?" Raegan said, lowering her chin and raising her eyebrows. "We're in public. Grow up."

"So he canceled on you?" Clark asked. Unlike the others, Clark looked genuinely concerned.

Before I could answer, the youngest of the three spoke up. "Wait, that worthless piece of shit cancelled on you?" Coby said. The boys were all only eleven months apart, making Coby just eighteen. My coworkers knew my brothers had all scored fake IDs and thought they were doing me a favor by looking the other way, but most of the time I wished they wouldn't. Coby in particular still acted like a twelve-year-old boy not quite sure what to do with his testosterone. He was bowing up behind the others, letting them hold him back from a fight that didn't exist.

"What are you doing, Coby?" I asked. "He's not even here!"

"You're damn right he's not," Coby said. He relaxed, cracking his neck. "Canceling on my baby sister. I'll bust his fuckin' face." I thought about Coby and T.J. getting into a brawl, and it made my heart race. T.J. was intimidating when he was younger, and lethal as an adult. No one fucked with him, and Coby knew it.

A disgusted noise came from my throat, and I rolled my eyes. "Just…find another table."

All four boys pulled chairs around Raegan and me. Colin had light-brown hair, but my brothers were all redheads. Colin and Chase had blue eyes. Clark and Coby had green. Some redheaded men aren't all that great-looking, but my brothers were tall, chiseled, and outgoing. Clark was the only one with freckles, and they still somehow looked good on him. I was the outcast, the only child with mousy brown hair and big, round, light blue eyes. More than once the boys tried to convince me that I'd been adopted. If I wasn't the female version of my father, I might have believed them.

I touched my forehead to the table and groaned. "I can't believe it, but this day just got worse."

"Aw, c'mon, Camille. You know you love us," Clark said, nudging me with his shoulder. When I didn't answer, he leaned in to whisper in my ear. "You sure you're all right?"

I kept my head down, but nodded. Clark patted my back a couple of times, and then the table grew quiet.

I lifted my head. Everyone was staring behind me, so I turned around. Trenton Maddox was standing there, holding two shot glasses and another glass of something that looked decidedly less sweet.

"This table turned into a party fast," Trenton said with a surprised but charming smile.

Chase narrowed his eyes at Trenton. "Is that him?" he asked, nodding.

"What?" Trenton asked.

Coby's knee began to bounce, and he leaned forward in his chair. "That's him. He fuckin' canceled on her, and then he showed up here."

"Wait. Coby, no," I said, holding up my hands.

Coby stood up. "You jackin' with our sister?"

"Sister?" Trenton said, his eyes bouncing between me and the volatile gingers sitting on each side of me.

"Oh, God," I said, closing my eyes. "Colin, tell Coby to stop. It's not him."

"Who's not me?" Trenton said. "We got a problem here?"

Travis appeared at his brother's side. He wore the same amused expression as Trenton, both flashing their matching left-sided dimples. They could have been their mother's second set of twins. Only subtle differences set them apart, including the fact that Travis was maybe an inch or two taller than Trenton.

Travis crossed his arms across his chest, making his already large biceps bulge. The only thing that kept me from exploding from my chair was that his shoulders relaxed. He wasn't ready to fight. Yet.

"Evening," Travis said.

The Maddoxes could sense trouble. At least it seemed that way, because whenever there was a fight, they had either started it, or finished it. Usually both.

"Coby, sit down," I commanded through my teeth.

"No, I'm not sittin' down. This dickhead insulted my sister, I'm not fuckin' sittin' down."

Raegan leaned over to Chase. "That's Trent and Travis Maddox."

"Maddox?" Clark asked.

"Yeah. You still got something to say?" Travis said.

Coby shook his head slowly and smiled. "I can talk all night long, motherfu—"

I stood. "Coby! Sit your ass down!" I said, pointing to his chair. He sat. "I said it wasn't him, and I meant it! Now everybody *calm* the *fuck* down! I've had a *bad* day, I'm here to drink, and relax, and have a good *goddamn* time! Now if that's a problem for you, back the fuck off my table!" I closed my eyes and screamed the last part, looking completely insane. People around us were staring.

Breathing hard, I glanced at Trenton, who handed me a drink.

One corner of his mouth turned up. "I think I'll stay."

acknowledgments

As always, thank you to my darling, patient husband. Without him, the many hours I put into my job would not be possible. We've molded our lives around my new career, and we've become a well-oiled machine. Thank you, love.

Thank you to my children for their patience, understanding, and for not making me feel too guilty for the evenings, nights, and weekends I work to meet a deadline.

Thank you to Patty for the use of the Blackwell Dairy Queen.

Thank you to Theresa Wegand, Amy Tannenbaum, and Linda Roberts for their work on this novella, and to Kim Easton for beta reading.

Last but not least, thank you Danielle Lagasse and her MacPack for the amazing cheerleading, encouragement and promotional work they've done for my novels. I appreciate you all so very much!

Look for news, events, and upcoming works, including the next installment of the *Happenstance* series at www.jamiemcguire.com

about the author

Jamie McGuire was born in Tulsa, OK. She attended the Northern Oklahoma College, the University of Central Oklahoma, and Autry Technology Center where she graduated with a degree in Radiography.

Jamie paved the way for the New Adult genre with international bestseller, Beautiful Disaster. Her follow-up novel Walking Disaster debuted at #1 on the New York Times, USA Today, and Wall Street Journal bestseller lists. She has also written apocalyptic thriller Red Hill, a novella titled A Beautiful Wedding, and the Providence series, a young adult paranormal romance trilogy.

Jamie now lives on a ranch just outside Enid, OK with husband Jeff, and their three children. They share their thirty acres with cattle, six horses, three dogs, and Rooster the cat.

here's where you can find jamie:

www.jamiemcguire.com

https://www.facebook.com/Jamie.McGuire.Author

twitter: @JamieMcGuire

instagram: JamieMcGuire_

29078009R00121

Made in the USA
Middletown, DE
07 February 2016